Cossayuna Lake

Andrien Beck

Special Thanks to Emilee & Shannon

Cover art (woman's face) painted by Marie Wells

PART 1

Chapter 1

The four thousand-square-foot log cabin was constructed in the early 1900s by Lemuel Gordon. The history surrounding the property weaved between the folklore of sacrificial blood and the Second Great Awakening. The lake became part of the burned-over district, the mass of its population inhabited by nothing more than superstitious zealots. Kelcy's beliefs wobbled somewhere between truth and folklore. There was a long history of dark things existing centuries before someone leveled the cabin's foundation. Cossayuna was a secluded lake and one of the main reasons she took the offer to move back. Spending the first eighteen years of her life watching its shorelines, she vowed to never come back. Her childhood memories were nothing but disastrous, and it took a darker tragedy to drag her back. When Kelcy had given birth to her child, the idea of losing stability, whether that be financial or mental, was something that happened to other people. Or so she thought. Maybe the familiarity of the land and slow-paced neighboring towns could be a good place for them to start over. Several years passed since any locals had seen her, and Kelcy considered that a blessing. The townsfolk didn't know her story, and it would give them a fighting chance to paint their narrative. The privacy of the lake provided additional security, and Kelcy considered that a big plus. They couldn't stay in Seattle anymore. A threatened disability claim hammered the final nail in that coffin. It was her only source of income and security, despite the harm she went through to get it.

Her father inherited the cabin from her great-grandfather Josephus. She never met her great grandfather, but the old black and white photos that clung to the hallway walls, encased in crusty old black metal frames, were scary looking enough to heed any investigation. He owned a local fishery in the nineteen-twenties, providing bait and cleaning services to the anglers and tourists who visited the lake during the summer and winter months. When the snow fell, he hosted ski excursions across the frozen lake, offsetting the little cleaning work he would get from ice fishing. It was a very successful business until the murders of nineteen forty-two. One important piece of information, a known local fact, surrounding the incident was that Josephus was a drunk. Some locals claimed parts of his testimony were nothing more than the ramblings of a town drunkard. No one would say that to the man's face if they had an inkling of intelligence, but his addiction was well documented. The reputation did not include violence, however. Outside of his ailment, the townsfolk knew him as a loving father and husband. This single detail surged the multiple rumors and oddness surrounding the incident. It was the winter of that year, and Josephus had led a group of vacationers on a ski excursion around the lake. As always, he would circle the south side, cutting through the middle, where the anglers set camp. Out-of-towners, mostly city folk, would travel from all around to lean over the holes and stare into the depths of the frozen abyss. Kelcy could never understand the curiosity of digging into the frozen lake and sitting around for hours hoping to catch nasty lake trout. It was a pastime that she considered gross. All that blood and guts. Back then, on a clear day, when you looked out over the lake, you could see the big red patches where the anglers would clean their catch. Josephus would lecture them, offering his service at a cheaper rate, so they would stop leaving the guts on the ice. It made the vacationers uncomfortable and they would avoid the lake tours. Who would want their children to see all the gore? The anglers continued the tradition, ignoring her great-grandad. They still cut the fish on the ice, and as a child, Kelcy would skit out to the abandoned holes with a few neighboring children and stare at the remains. Someone would make the dare to scrape the entrails to the edge, and if brave enough, peer down into the black depth of the lake. Kelcy was always the one to kick them in, watching the blobs of entrails float like jellyfish, suspended in animation, sinking into obscurity. She hadn't feared the lake. At least back then.

They deemed the incident of forty-two as an accident. The authorities didn't believe the sixty-five-year-old man could have slaughtered the vacationers. The tour approached the unoccupied holes sometime around midafternoon. The news reported strong winds on the lake, causing flurries, and creating low visibility. Even if a skilled angler went out there, they wouldn't have seen all the blood. When the conditions calmed, three anglers came back to the holes to find Josephus alone, sitting with his feet dangling knee-deep in the water. Each of the five holes harbored a set of ski poles in their drifts, and one, if not both, skis lying next to it. Blood stained the ice in large puddles, creating crimson Rorschach. Near the farthest hole to the East, they discovered the head of a young man. Several rumors began floating amongst the locals. One of which involved an angler approaching the severed head and spewing his lunch on the ice. Another included the dead man's mouth gaping open like a fish, screaming at the mountains in the distance. She heard the bellowing face was bullshit. Later in the year, someone said the police report included, upon further inspection, someone removed the screaming man's eyes and tongue.

When the authorities arrived, Josephus stated, "She took them. All of them." He reeked of alcohol, and they found an empty flask stuffed in his parka. An officer located a gutting knife covered in blood next to one of the other fishing holes. They discovered the victims' eviscerated bodies, hooked to fish stringers, submerged in the lake. Townsfolk believed some of the details to be more lore than fact because some of these descriptions are absent from any official documents. A trial took place that summer and the townsfolk trust those records lost as well. Kelcy assumed it was all wild accusations and folklore, not giving them any credit, given the opportunity to read them. Josephus received a not guilty verdict. His age had played a role in the decision, plus the lack of evidence. There were no fingerprints on the knife, and Josephus claimed *she* took them. Somehow, whoever *she* was, remained undetected on the ice. There was an enormous amount of questioning while they combed through the old man's ledgers and books. They found nothing serious out of order. After the investigation, they accounted for and confirmed the deaths of everyone but Josephus on that tour. If there was another person out there, the storm shielded their identity and Josephus was a lucky man. Authorities, with help from the surrounding townsfolk, conducted a large manhunt that lasted three months. Parents held their children captive, ruining the entire winter vacation. The gossip of the now dubbed Cossayuna Lake Killer gripped the community, and no child was to be alone. Especially on the lake.

During the following months, the manhunt ceased, and the newspapers, along with the late night news, reported less and less. By the next summer, the killer's fifteen minutes of fame ended. Every so often, the story would pop up. A reporter from a magazine would come asking questions. The locals would turn them away and go on about their business, tired of the drama. Josephus spent the rest of his life alone in the cabin, refusing to step foot near the lake. If someone spotted him walking around his property, he would wave and then head back inside. Most of the locals knew to leave well enough alone. His fishery closed, and when he died, Kelcy's grandfather inherited the property. Some townsfolk still questioned his innocence. The townsfolk became divided within a few decades. Some continued to support her great-grandfather, while others dubbed him the true Cossayuna Lake Killer. There was even talk of a family curse.

Kelcy had asked her dad why his father had never taken over the family business. "He was not allowed near that lake. None of us were," he told her. Josephus was a widower, and Kelcy knew nothing of her great-grandmother, except that she died a few years after her grandfather was born. Her great-grandfather had died a lonely man.

Her father started a bait and tackle shop in his younger twenties, but closed it after five seasons, moving to Chicago, where Kelcy was born. When she last spoke to her mother and father, they offered the cabin as a place to stay. To heal. Kelcy refused at first, but as the weeks passed, she realized she had no choice. During an afternoon walk, her parents convinced her it would be good for them to get away. The solitude would give her time to get back on her feet. Besides, this would be the fourth generation of Beckles to live in Cossayuna.

"Maybe we will get a road named after us." Her dad teased.

Kelcy went home and began packing that night. Panic climbed her neck as she rehearsed what she was going to say to her son. As a toddler, Seth hadn't formed strong friendships with other children, so the move was nothing more than another event in his brief life. But soon, she would need to stop all of this. The erratic lifestyle, the lack of money. The struggle. They deserved better. Sometimes negative thoughts would creep. Maybe her son needed more than what she could provide. Something better than her. They would watch television, snuggling in bed, and he would wrap his little arms around her neck and kiss her cheek. In those moments, she was all he needed.

His father, Bradley, was a tragic story. Overdosing backstage during a brief tour in Louisiana. A man with too much to lose and not enough care to realize it. His band had released their fourth album, and he pulled the rock star conversation on her, pleading that this would be his last tour for a while. He would come home, work on getting off the sauce, and spend every waking moment with them. She believed him, desperate to prove her parents wrong about him. They hated Bradley, and their feelings toward his disposition increased when she broke the news of her pregnancy. How would a druggy musician protect and financially support their daughter and grandson? He couldn't. Bradley lashed back with obscenities and binges that resulted in being forbidden from family functions. When he died, their son was an infant and her parents stepped in without judgment, supplying emotional and financial support. She worked extra hours to pay the bills, and her parents took their grandson as often as needed. She hated relying on them and although they swore she wasn't a burden, Kelcy felt differently. They already raised a child. This was supposed to be their time. There were days she looked out onto the lake and wished to disappear into one of those frozen fishing holes. Sink into the depths where she would disappoint no one. Her parents would raise Seth. Giving him more than she ever could. Maybe the second time around, her parents would have a child to be proud of. As quickly as these thoughts materialized, anger would rise from the bottom of her stomach, pulsating its way to her throat, escaping in a silent scream. Then it would pass. A repeating cycle.

    The first snow had fallen a few days prior, and the lake's white teeth bit the shoreline, eating the frozen trays jetting from the beach. Small white orbs fell from the trees, dancing their way to a blinding whitewash, now covering the yard. The black dirt of the road peeked through patches snaking along the lake line. Kelcy followed it until the dense treeline separating her property from her neighbors on the left. From the back of the cabin, she could hear the television. The faint high-pitched voice of SpongeBob telling his faithful companion they were indeed men. The corners of her mouth turned up, and she closed her eyes, envisioning him sitting in her lap, clapping his hands and singing. They had watched the movie so many times she had memorized the dialogue. *Now that we're men, we have facial hair. Now that we're men, I changed my underwear.* Kelcy laughed and watched the clouds recede in slow motion. The comical sound cut through the screen door and escaped out over the lake, and she wondered if they were listening. The bodies, long ago forgotten, ebbing in weeds and soil at the bottom of the lake. She rubbed her arms as the goosebumps pricked her skin. *There are no them,* her inner voice assured. *Kelcy, they buried them somewhere in town.* Little footsteps rushed up behind her, two tight grips embracing her legs. Kelcy looked at the top of his little mop of hair and smiled.

"Hi." He looked up at her. She reached down and lifted his weight to her hip as he wrapped his arms around her neck.

"What are you watchiking, Mommy?"

"Watching, honey," she corrected, snuggling him closer.

"Mommy is just enjoying the snow, Peapod." She looked out over the water and the bumps on her arms returned full force. The visage of the lake held an ominous emotion, capping and thrusting into black shadows. The lake held respect for a good reason. Bad things could happen out there. Not curses of local folklore and superstition. These were natural things. The world bit back when you angered what you should leave well enough alone.

Chapter 2: Bradley & The Boy

The Creek Tavern was not the type of bar that Kelcy would frequent. She preferred lounges with fancy drinks, high-end appetizers, and background music. Venues where you could talk without screaming. She held nothing against taverns, but they became too loud, and the clientele would indulge far past self control. Most of the bands that played the Creek were punk rock or of the metal variety. Massive parties would follow every show, fueled by drugs and large quantities of alcohol. You could attend, if you knew someone cool enough to invite you. Kelcy harbored no desire to be invited and didn't want to be seen in the Creek. Her friends were relentless. Resorting to cheap slander followed up with embarrassing laughter aimed at shaming her. In the end, she relented and didn't see the harm in one night. If anyone spotted her entering or leaving, she would claim it to be a blind dare, dropped off with her friends as a cruel joke.

  The parking lot was littered with motorcycles and old beat-up cars from the mid-eighties. A couple of girls dressed in short skirts, their tight midriffs showing from under crop tops, leaned against rough-looking machinery. One of the young blondes sported a jeweled belly button, and Kelcy tried not to roll her eyes. They swooned on rugged-looking men, with long dirty hair, smoking cigarettes and concealing bottles behind their thighs as they leaned against their rides. When they entered the bar, the smell hit her in the face like a two-ton brick. Sweat, cheap cologne, and spicy perfume mixed with the faint odor of vomit made Kelcy gag. Her friends laughed, holding out their wrists to a heavy set hairy man sporting a skull tattoo on the side of his shaved head. He eyed her friends up and down with a smirk, stamped their hands without checking their ID, and ushered them along. The doorman paused, giving Kelcy an odd look before asking her for ID. She looked at him and pointed at her friends.

"Protocol." he laughed.

Kelcy unzipped her clutch and fished out her license. He studied the hard plastic for a moment and made a scoffing sound before handing it back to her. She wanted to slap him across the face. Tell him what a shit hole this place was before stomping out. He looked like the kind that wouldn't have it, so she kept her mouth shut and stuffed the ID back in her purse.

"Watch your ass, kid," he winked and stamped her wrist.

"You ain't the type to be in here," he added, and Kelcy scrunched her nose up as he moved on to the next group in line, stamping them with no ID check. She rolled her eyes and caught up with her friends, who were in the process of lining the bar with shots. She listened to them hoot and holler as the bartender went down the line. Kelcy wondered what drew her to be friends with them. It certainly wasn't any of this. Maybe that's why HR advised using the word acquaintance for co-workers. The shrill of amplified feedback burst from the far end of the bar, followed by a high-pitched yell. A tall, scrawny man gripped a microphone as he teetered over the edge of the stage.

"Back from their Florida tour." He swayed, his right foot resting on the monitor speaker.

"The local bad boys from Kinny Peaks, The Rebels' Dominion!"

The crowd erupted and raced toward the stage, beer bottles raised above their heads. Her friends continued downing shots as Kelcy eyed each band member as they took the stage. The frail announcer handed his microphone to the frontman and hopped over the monitor, joining the forming crowd in the front row. The leader, dressed in all black, had tattoos covering both arms with depictions of fire, razors, erotic women, and tribal designs.

He cupped the microphone, raising it to his mouth. "You ready for some crazy bullshit tonight, Kinny Peaks?"

The crowd roared, sloshing alcohol over their heads while pumping their fists.

"On drums," he turned, pointing at the back of the stage, "Hailing from Minnesota, Kenny Skins Holland!"

The booming sound of war drums filled the room as the drummer flailed his arms, beating his instrument before standing up and tossing a stick toward the crowd. The singer pumped his fist and walked over toward the right side of the stage.

"On bass, all the way from three blocks away." The crowd broke into laughter and the bassist bowed, giving the crowd a wicked smile.

"Jimmie Low End Brewer!" Jimmie slid his hand down the neck and a distorted grumble filled the bar.

A bottle vibrated on an abandoned table nearby and Kelcy folded her arms, contemplating sneaking away and going home. A small headache grew behind her eyes and there was no way she could make it through an entire set of this nonsense. The singer put his fingers to his lips, and the crowd simmered down.

"And last but never least," he held out his hand, pointing to the left side of the stage. Kelcy twisted her mouth as a spotlight illuminated an empty mic stand.

"The one and only, Kinny Peaks own, Bradley Six Strings Caldwell!"

The crowd erupted into a frenzy as Bradley stepped from the shadows and stomped on his pedal board, delivering a sharp series of notes that threatened to shatter Kelcy's eardrums. Her eyes vibrated, widening as she watched his sweaty body glisten under the crude stage lighting. Canned hues of red and blue mixed with his black leather vest. Long brown hair, as if numb to the effects of gravity, swam through the air in slow motion, ebbing in the contrasting light show. Kelcy took baby steps toward the stage. As she entered the crowd, they seemed to part for her, understanding her awe-struck nature. She approached the stage, looking up at him as if he were a God. Bradley looked down and winked as the note faded. For the entire set, they played cat and mouse. She would bat her lashes, the coy smile as if she knew nothing but innocence. Bradley winked and showed his teeth like a lion, emphasizing notes while gyrating his hips. When the show was over, she waited around for the crowd to clear. The girls left without saying goodbye, and Kelcy couldn't care less. She would find a way home. Bradley was on the stage packing gear when she leaned across the railing and smiled. He abandoned the cable he was rolling and gave her a wicked grin.

When she told him she was pregnant two years later, Bradley was unfazed by the news. Grabbing her in a bear hug, he squeezed her so hard she let out a small grunt. He pulled away and stared at her belly.

"I am sorry!" he put his hands around her waist, careful not to compress her stomach. She hesitated, telling him. This was going to change everything for them. For him especially. What if he became upset? She didn't want this to affect his dreams of playing music. Bradley was gone a lot on tour, and the trips would need to be planned further in advance. As the months progressed, she would expect him to take some time off for her and the baby. He didn't object to any of it, telling the band at the following practice. They all got excited, slapping him on the back and taking him out for beers.

"A little Six String!" The singer told the crowd at The Creek. Everyone cheered and congratulated Kelcy, who sat barside, perched on a stool with a glass of water. She stopped hanging out with the girls, or rather, the other way around. She couldn't drink anymore and they didn't like Bradley, so the decision was easy, she supposed. They said he was gross and that it was one thing to see the band, but who wanted to date a poor musician? They averted their eyes, leaving the break room, continuing with hushed insults. Now that she was pregnant, they even stopped talking to her at lunch.

At first, the rumors about Bradley doing drugs were nothing more than that. She took it with a grain of salt. She accepted it as the assumed reputation in his line of work. It was always accusations of drugs, cheating, Satan worship, or all three. She was one hundred percent certain the last two were nothing to show concern over. She thought maybe she was wrong about the cheating when he started coming home and collapsing into bed without speaking to her. It was the first time in her life she hoped for Satanism. The morning she found him in the bathroom, those concerns became a reality. Her heart locked in her chest like a seized engine. Getting up late for work, Kelcy had rushed out the door, forgetting her lunch. She returned, pausing as she snatched her lunch bag from the counter. Calling for Bradley, she bounced into the living room to say goodbye and steal another kiss. He wasn't there. Searching the house, she called his name, each yell sounding a bit more angry. When she opened the bathroom door, the world pulled the rug from under her feet. His body lay slumped against the sink cabinet. Arms at his sides. He looked dead. Kelcy panicked, running to the kitchen and dumping her purse on the counter. She snatched her phone and raced back to the bathroom, calling 911. Vomit dribbled down his chin, from his blue lips, into a growing puddle on his chest. Kelcy stayed on the phone until the paramedics arrived.

 She felt betrayed when the doctor reported it was drug related. Heroin. He sat in the hospital bed, staring at his feet, refusing to speak. She didn't question why, or place blame, although she wanted to. Kelcy pushed her emotions down and cleared her mind so she could be there for him. Regardless of the why and the how. His parents were nonexistent, and now her parents ignored his cry for help. They were on their own. Kelcy's father expressed his outrage, telling her he was an embarrassment. Then, they pushed him out of the family. Kelcy blamed his continued use on her father for a long time. If they would have helped, maybe Bradley could have healed. Change. He continued to play out with the band. Calling her either high or intoxicated from the back of their van or some hotel. As her baby grew, so did his addictions, and when she gave birth, Bradley lay passed out on their living room floor, unresponsive and absent.

    Kelcy received a call from the police informing her they had discovered his body at a hotel in Louisiana. She showed no signs of tears. It was only a matter of time before she would receive that call, and everyone expected it. Her parents did their best to stand by her. Coworkers averted their eyes when she walked past. There was no funeral. She didn't want one. Kelcy picked up his ashes a week later. That afternoon, in the parking lot of their apartment, she wept as the sun bent over the top of the complex. The urn, fastened in the passenger seat, absorbed the heat from the windshield. Every dream she could have imagined had eroded. Kelcy sat, waiting for the sun to fade behind the brick facade of their once happy life. Tucking the urn in the crook of her arm, she walked toward the dumpster at the foot of the parking garage. Setting Bradley on the ground,

Kelcy lifted its heavy lid and peered inside. A waft of rot and decay plumed from the canister, and she picked up the urn and ran her fingers across the etched steel design. Taking a deep breath, she tossed it into the trash and walked away.

Chapter 3: Summer at the Cabin

Growing up in the city wasn't an ideal situation for a child. Kelcy's dad received a job promotion, and outside of that, she had limited knowledge surrounding their ability to afford a summer home. She only knew he made good money and his occupation had something to do with steel. Work consumed her father, and Kelcy didn't understand it back then, but it assured their family would never want for anything. He took extreme pride in that fact. Twice a year, every summer and winter, they would escape to the family cabin. Cossayuna Lake lay in the Southern Washington township in New York between the farming town of Argyle and the village of Greenwich. The village had a few claims to fame, the biggest one being a famous country singer by the name of Hal Ketchum. When her father would hear *Small Town Saturday night,* on the radio, he would point and say, "You know, that guy is from Greenwich!" Kelcy had no interest in country music, but she would raise her eyebrows and nod her head as if enlightened. Kelcy's mom spent most of her time in the kitchen or cleaning the cabin, while her dad worked from the phone in their cabin bedroom. Kelcy ended up fishing, swimming, and hiking alone, despite all the promises made. Truth be told, she didn't mind.

It allowed her time to explore the woods. She would spy on nearby houses like she was a secret agent, creating obscure missions in her head. *You must capture a description of the bearded man at the bottom of the hill. He is a known killer and double agent.* Kelcy would listen for the bellowing call of her mother to come get lunch. She would rush home and devour a few sandwiches before returning to her missions. Sometimes, she would come across strangers walking on the road. Most of the time, they were elderly folk out for casual exercise, passing each other with little more than a wave and a smile. Maybe even a hello if they knew and liked her family. This was lake life. Until it wasn't.

Kelcy was lounging on the dock, ankles bobbing in the water, when she first heard of the Cossayuna Lake Killer. She leaned back, watching the glass surface of the lake reflect the clouds when a boy in an oversized canoe floated by. He paused, eyeing her with suspicion.

"You live up there?" he shouted, nodding his head toward the hill. She nodded back as he paddled closer.

Resting the oar across his lap, he spit over the side of the canoe. "How long you live there?" He asked, dipping his hand in the water.

"Every summer since I can remember," she smiled. "Used to be my great grandpa's."

He scratched his head and stared at the cabin. "Josephus, your great grandad?" he asked, not taking his eyes from the structure on the hill.

"Yup." Kelcy swung her feet in and out of the water, only half listening to the conversation.

"You know who he is, or, uh, was, right?" He picked up his paddle and dipped it in the water, pushing the canoe back to put some distance between them. She looked up at him and shook her head no.

"He was the Cossayuna Lake Killer." He rested the paddle across his lap again and stared hard at her.

"What are you talking about?" She pulled her legs from the water and stood up, leaning over the edge of the dock.

"Ain't gonna tell a lie," he nodded. "I could see why your parents might not share that information with ya. But everyone around here knows, is all I'm saying. Ask your folks." He dipped his paddle and looked back toward the cabin. Nodding, he paddled off toward the middle of the lake. Kelcy watched him for a few minutes before turning and heading up the hill. She stormed into the kitchen, her arms folded tight across her chest. Her parents were sitting at the table having a cup of coffee, enjoying the silence. Kelcy took a few steps closer and looked back and forth between them.

"Was great grandpa the Cossayuna Lake Killer?" She questioned. Her father raised his eyebrows as her mother placed her cup on a napkin and gave Kelcy an exaggerated look of confusion.

Chapter 4: Baby Boy

Seth was born screaming like most babies. The blood-curdling screech caused Kelcy's heart to race. Was he ok? She tried to see what the nurses holding him down on the little steel table were doing. Within a few seconds, the screams turned to yelps, and the nurse rushed over to Kelcy, placing him on her chest, wrapped in a thin, blue-striped blanket. There was no time to be concerned about Bradley's absence as she held her new baby boy, crying as he stared into her eyes. His little dark orbs mirrored her reflection, and when he blinked, the antibiotic ointment clumped to his tiny eyelashes.

"Seth," she cooed.

Her mother leaned in and cupped the top of her grandson's head.

"Seth?" She let out a giggle. "So perfect."

Kelcy let out a snort, sobbing as the two mothers embraced the fresh addition to their bloodline. The doctors came and went, offering congratulations and checking on the new mother and baby. It was around one in the morning when Kelcy gave up on Bradley. No one had offered any condolences or asked where he was. She lay in bed, wondering, with the hospital crib next to her.

"It might be just us now, Peapod," she whispered over the rail.

Seth cooed, twisting his tiny hands and making little popping sounds with his heart-shaped mouth. Kelcy leaned up on her elbows and stared at him. A sudden fear made her heartache. The responsibility of bringing a human into the world alone made her breath catch in her throat. Even if Bradley got the help he needed, she knew in her heart that he would never be what their son needed. Kelcy lay in the hospital that night, staring at the ceiling and listening to her son's breathing. The world she had become accustomed to had forever changed, and as scary as it was, it was beautiful.

She stood in the cabin's kitchen watching Seth eat ravioli. He was always so happy, and she felt guilty not warning him about what this world could do. The damage of a conversation. Four years went by in the blink of an eye, and he was getting so big. *Four years without him.* The thought would sneak up from the depths of her mind, filling her with a sadness so deep it would paralyze her limbs. Seth was her consolation, and she held that close to her heart. There was an additional worry that plagued her now. They were living in a place filled with dark rumors about her family. Those stories needed to stay buried. Her child didn't need to know the folklore of the lake. The stories scorch their family name. Rumors can ruin things. Destroy lives. How did lies so horrid stretch so many years? Manifesting into monstrous fables aimed at defaming her family? She put the edge of her thumb into her mouth and gnawed at a hangnail. Seth tilted his head and nibbled at the beef-filled pasta, smiling and humming as he stared into his bowl. She remembered being innocent like that. Before the boy in the canoe. Kelcy wished she had never stomped into the kitchen, asking about her great-grandpa. Did people still talk about it? In some places, gossip was like history. It had a way of repeating itself. Hurting and destroying people. Keeping things rotten. People's mouths dig up buried things we should leave alone. Things like her great-grandfather.

"All done Mommy." Seth looked up, his chin covered in amber-colored sauce. Kelcy smiled, taking the washcloth from the sink and turning on the faucet. She bent down to wipe his face, and he retracted, giggling as she pretended to fight him.

"Let me get you." She lowered her voice like a monster. Seth burst into laughter, relenting to her onslaught. Finishing, she stood and turned, tossing the washcloth into the metal basin.

"She took them." Seth giggled.

Kelcy's heart thumped in her chest, and she spun around, staring down at Seth.

"What did you just say, Peapod?" Her voice was tight.

Seth looked up at her and giggled again. He hopped down from his seat and jogged in place as if he was about to sprint away.

"What did you say, Peapod?" she asked again, bending down, holding his hands. Seth looked out at the television in the living room and pulled his hands away, pointing.

"He shook him, Mommy." His eyes brightened.

Kelcy watched as the big sheepdog grabbed the coyote by the neck, shook him, and then bopped him on the head. The dazed coyote wobbled as a flesh-colored lump formed on the crest of his skull.

Chapter 5: Off the Beaten Path

A luxury afflicting Kelcy's guilt was the nanny her parents employed to help with Seth. She objected to the idea, but being alone at the cabin, her mother insisted. The company became a godsend. As much as she loved her son, she needed some adult conversation. Something more than the lives of cartoon characters. The nanny inquired about what Kelcy did for employment, but the conversation became short-lived when she explained her workplace accident and subsequent disability claim. The stranger didn't press, and so Kelcy didn't divulge the accident had been her fault. She lost her temper, arguing with the billing department about the pending shipping costs, and stormed out of the bay. She would have noticed the new sign and the steep drop-off at the end of the step-up if she had calmed down. On autopilot, she walked right off the edge, lucky to receive only a torn MCL. Kelcy thought her knee would heal after a few months of therapy and she could return to work. Then they proposed surgery. As luck would have it, her knee never healed correctly, and it had become too difficult to walk upstairs or travel for meetings. Her job claimed her unfit for work, and that was that. They let her go without so much as a goodbye. Seth was only a little over one year old. How would she support her child? Her father hired a lawyer who inquired about existing surveillance at the facility. Learning there were no cameras installed on that side of the building, he recommended she pursue a disability lawsuit. The money lasted until her therapy proved her fit to work. She then lived off her awarded pain and suffering payment until it dwindled to nothing.

    Miss Brendle, who refused to be called anything but Becky, helped Kelcy with everyday chores. When Kelcy felt weak or stressed, Becky took Seth out for walks or to the store to get snacks. Fear would paralyze Kelcy every time they headed down the drive. She counted the minutes until they returned, running to the door and waiting for him to emerge from the backseat of Becky's car. When Seth took his afternoon nap, they would sit on the front porch, looking out over the lake, and talk about small things. Books they were interested in reading, or favorite shows growing up. When Kelcy wanted to pry, she would ask Becky personal questions. This would lead to her real interests. How she met her family. She claimed to know limited information. Kelcy's parents had contacted her through a temp agency. Honestly, she didn't think she was going to get the job because of the way her father acted uninterested towards her during the interview. Kelcy sympathized, telling Becky it wasn't her. It was part of his demeanor when it involved business and family. They had surprised Becky a week later by leaving a message on her answering machine, asking when she could start. Kelcy raised an eyebrow and reiterated that they were just being overprotective. Becky hadn't taken offense and laughed it off, viewing it as part of getting the gig.

"Have you heard the stories about this lake?" Kelcy sipped her tea, looking out over the water. Becky shook her head, setting her teacup on the arm of her chair.

"As in what, exactly?" She leaned in, heavily interested in local gossip.

Kelcy took another sip and measured how to proceed. Was there a tactful way to mention the history of the lake? It's folklore. She assumed there would be no delicate way of talking about murder. Kelcy looked over towards the neighbor's yard. A tall pine swayed above its lot, bending towards the lake. Kelcy smiled, looking into the abyss of her mug. There was more than murder here. This lake had a deep native history. Contrary to the rumors, the soil contained no sacrificial blood. Kelcy weighed the consequences of indulging in the details about the murders. Would Becky think she was crazy?

Run back to her father, refusing to work for a nut job? Kelcy would have to leave her family's name out of it for now. Biting into her bottom lip, she took a slow, deep breath.

"There was a murder back in the forties." Kelcy studied her cup before taking another sip.

Becky's eyes widened, and she shuffled in her chair to get comfortable. *So much for being considered a nut job.* Kelcy looked out over the lake and watched the surface turn to glass, reflecting the sky as if to hide itself.

"The anglers found bodies under the ice." She pointed to the depths and looked over at Becky with a small grin.

Her anxiety eased as Becky gave her a wicked smile. "It was winter, and the anglers had their fishing holes drilled." She continued nursing her cup. "Bodies of tourists were gutted and tied to stringers."

"Stringers?" Becky interrupted. The confused look on her face almost made Kelcy laugh.

"It's what you tie fish to as you catch them." She explained. "You hang it in the water so they can stay alive but can't swim away."

Becky's face contorted as she turned her gaze toward the lake.

"They were on the ice for a lake tour." Kelcy continued, sipping and smacking her lips together.

Becky huffed, looking over at Kelcy. In a low voice, she whispered. "Why would they be skiing on the lake?"

"Well," Kelcy shifted in her chair. "That was quite the pastime. People loved this place and traveled from all around the world to see it." She paused, looking Becky dead in the eyes. "There was a head found on the ice near one hole. It's eyes and tongue missing."

Becky covered her mouth and giggled. Kelcy grinned, feeling a small ping of anxiety claw its way up her chest as she continued.

"The police conducted a search party, but it ended in nothing, and they never captured the killer."

Kelcy leaned over, giving Becky a childish grin.

"So," she stared deep into her eyes. "Still want to stick around?"

Becky's mouth hung ajar, and she looked down at her teacup. Scanning over the lake, she faced Kelcy, taking a deep breath.

"Fuck yeah!" She broke into laughter. "This is like one of those old horror films!" Her eyes widened, expressing excitement. "Like Sleepaway Camp!"

Kelcy nodded, trying not to express how relieved she was. She settled back in her seat and relaxed. The anxiety nestled itself in the pit of her stomach, dissolving into her lower back. Her tea had grown cold, so she placed the cup on the arm of her chair and considered abandoning it.

"Never seen that one." She tapped her finger against the armrest.

Becky nodded and made a slight frown. "Wow, you are missing out!" She sipped from her cup, making an exaggerated slurping sound.

There was silence between them for a moment, and Kelcy closed her eyes. The conversation had stirred up thoughts of Bradley, and her heart ached. The lake was still. As if it were listening. Indulging in her sadness. She looked again at the large swaying pine in the adjacent lot. Her mouth opened, and before she could stop herself, the words spilled forward.

"What do you think happens when you die?" She said, looking up at the tree before turning to gauge Becky's response.

Becky's face tightened as if she had eaten something sour.

"I don't know?" Shrugging her shoulders as she scans the lake. "I mean, Heaven maybe, if you believe that sort of thing?" Becky reached across and took hold of Kelcy's hand. "Your parents told me a little about what happened. I'm sorry."

Kelcy's throat clenched, and she realized this conversation might get back to her parents. They would come screaming, demanding her to go back to therapy. She looked into her lap as a lump formed in her throat.

Becky let go of her hand and leaned back in her chair. "Well," she softened her voice, "It's okay to talk about it, Kelcy. It's healthy. It will be just between us, okay?"

Kelcy leaned back in her seat and struggled to keep the tears from coming. Becky looked over and studied Kelcy's face. "You know," she sat up and shifted her weight in her seat. "We should talk about something else, huh?"

Kelcy nodded and put on a fake smile. Becky stuck the tip of her tongue out between her teeth. "So what are your thoughts on Henry Cavill?" Kelcy flopped her head towards Becky and rolled her eyes before letting out a small laugh.

Chapter 6: When The Dead Are Talking

It started as a dream. Loud music boomed as the crowd raved. An ocean of bodies swaying to a grinding tempo that at one time would have annoyed Kelcy. The Rebels' Dominion was on their second set and Bradley put his hand to his brow and scanned the audience. Weaving between raving fans, Kelcy peeked her head up every so often to keep her direction. She wanted to sneak up, surprising him at the front row railing. The staff loved her and turned a blind eye to the antics she pulled trying to get his attention. Even Paul, the greasy doorman, who had once ID'd her with suspicion, now smiled and rolled his eyes at her nonsense. It was her duty to fuck up his show. To pull his attention away just long enough to mess up his groove. It was a harmless game they played every night, and the band never complained, insisting that it made the show more fun. They distracted him while she propped herself front row and pulled her shirt up, exposing herself to him when he spun around. The singer would laugh, jumbling his lyrics as Bradley grabbed her by the waist and yanked her onto the stage. He would kiss her and yell, "I love this chick!" as the band raged on with no guitarist. She would awaken to shadows dancing on the ceiling as the music faded. Several times a week, Kelcy would stand at Seth's door and watch him sleep, wondering how she was going to make this work.

Towards the end, she stopped going to his shows. A lot of people did. She wouldn't dare say it, but their fifteen minutes of fame in that small town had run out. There was another rising local band, with much younger and thinner members, called The Bottom Creek Boys. They played all the new-age country music, and the local girls loved them. Everyone in that business knows that where the girls go, the boys will follow. The lack of gigs made their income tight. Bradley divided any money he brought in between his drug habit and his actual responsibilities. Kelcy devoted every dime to their family, often going without necessary personal items. She got those by stealing from her mother's house while using their bathroom. There was no doubt her mother was aware of the theft. The stock of sanitary items and toiletries became larger over the remaining months of his life. When Bradley died, the stock dwindled to her mother's expectations. It was not her parents' problem that Bradley was gone. When her financial woes increased, they stepped in again, assuming Bradley had left her nothing, and they were right. After the accident, Kelcy could no longer afford to take care of her son, and the time to be proud was over.

Late at night, while Seth was asleep, Bradley would talk to her from the dark corners of their bedroom. At first, she thought she was losing her mind. His voice was so vivid. He would tell her how proud he was. How well she was doing with their son, and that he was sorry for the choices he had made that took him away. She cursed him under her breath, and he moaned, accepting her profanity as penance. Bradley would only manifest at the height of her anxiety. When she felt she might snap. That pattern made her concerned about her sanity. She would lie in bed pressing her hand to her chest and he would slither from the recesses of their dark room, trying to calm her with his apologies. She had shared the occurrences with her therapist, and the doctor determined it to be a necessary coping mechanism. The visits had been the only thing that could settle her racing thoughts. Help her get through another day. Kelcy refused the medication that was prescribed to her. It was poison. She needed to be stronger for Seth, not clouded with drugs. Kelcy called the therapist's office and canceled all appointments. The day before they moved to the cabin, Bradley snaked across the bedroom, his presence nothing more than a faint whisper. She strained to hear his breath sliding over the floorboards. Approaching the bedside, he paused just below where her head lay.

Do you want to go? He asked. The tone in his voice was deep and concerned.

She faced the other side of the room and closed her eyes. "Do we have a choice, Bradley? You left us. We have nothing now."

Kelcy could sense him pulling the sheets taut, climbing the side of the bed. The apparition pressed up against her back, and she trembled, fear spiking as he caressed her neck.

If you leave, I cannot follow you. He sighed.

Kelcy held her breath and let him run his phantom fingers through her hair. She wasn't sure how she felt anymore. Would she be better off without him? Maybe taking Seth away and starting a new life was a mistake. Seth deserved better than this. A life without ghosts and sad memories?

You don't mean that. He groaned. His voice held a pain she had never heard before. The slithering vocals rattled with stress. But she did. She meant it. Bradley slid from behind her to the floor, his breath ragged and weak.

I have always loved you, Kelcy. He whimpered.

Tears streamed down her face as she listened to his breathing fade deeper and deeper into the shadows. Her respirations locked in unison with his, growing weaker and weaker until she almost choked. The air burned her throat as she gasped. As the room fell silent, Kelcy moaned, hugging her pillow as she sobbed. Her heart slammed against her rib cage. Both manic with sorrow and relief from his release.

Chapter 7: The Walkabout

The next day, when Becky arrived, Kelcy had informed her she was going to take a walk along the lake shore. Her anxiety had eased over the last few months, and she had come to grips with trusting Becky with Seth's safety. Kelcy would help her get things situated, and then she would be off to take a few moments for herself. Try to figure out what the hell she was going to do about their future. They couldn't live in the cabin forever, although her parents would not object. Kelcy wasn't interested in becoming a prisoner again, even if it lifted her financial burdens. Nothing was worth feeling trapped. Seth was playing at the kitchen table when Becky walked in, draping her summer jacket over the chair. She bent down next to him and nudged his arm. "Whatcha doin' big guy?"

He tilted his head to the side and gave her a playful look before returning to his blocks. Becky stood up and went to the sink to wash her hands as Kelcy looked out the front door toward the lake, scanning the surface of the water.

"You excited?" Becky asked as she pumped a liberal amount of hand soap before scrubbing her hands under the faucet. Kelcy kept her gaze on the ebbing water and studied the shoreline as if she were looking for something.

"Ya." Kelcy relaxed her shoulders. "I think it will be good."

Becky let out a chuckle and dried her hands with the dish rag hanging from the sink cabinet. "Yeah, of course it will." She pulled the chair next to Seth and looked over the blocks he had assembled into a nonsensical stack. "What do we have here, bud?" She teased him, nudging his shoulder again. Seth let out a giggle and nudged her back.

"House!" He chirped, as he continued to add blocks to the multicolored tower. Becky nodded and joined in, making her makeshift dwelling. Kelcy smiled and leaned into the front door, looking out of the screen mesh as she tapped on the door frame.

"You behave for Miss Becky." She called back to them. Seth looked up and shook his head. The simplicity of his world amazed her. Children have no sense of fear, even when it is imminent. The inability to taste what's coming. Kelcy left them to play and headed down the drive to the edge of the road. She looked back up at the cabin, staring at the windows above the kitchen. What room once belonged to Josephus? Which window did he sit at during his last days? There was no need to indulge in old folklore, and she pushed back the unhealthy thoughts. But she knew that sometimes thoughts needed to be unhealthy. It exposed the truth, and Kelcy wanted to learn what that truth was, even if it took her down a terrible road. The stories about what transpired that day on the ice didn't sit well with her, and she needed to figure out why. She didn't believe the rumors were true about Josephus, but there were unknown details. Her father avoided talking about his dad or grandad, and she felt he was harboring some kind of guilt. When she would ask questions, her father would shake his head and say, "You know your grandparents. They kept to themselves." He claimed to spend very little time with his grandfather, but she saw the pictures that once lined the walls of the cabin. Several of them had been of her father sitting on her great-granddad's lap, eating an apple or piece of candy. The old man's maniacal smile seemed twisted and hurt as he stared into the camera. It made Kelcy uncomfortable. From what she had read in the newspaper accounts, Josephus was a peaceful man. He wasn't a churchgoer, none of her family was, but he was not the type of guy to start a problem. "The man accepted people at face value," her father would say.

"Just a hard-working fool." He added, "Like your dad." He would add a wink as if that smoothed things over.

He drank. That was his poison. Everyone harbored poison. Kelcy thought about Bradley and wondered if he was hers. The child sitting on his lap in those photos was impervious to what might have lived within the old man. He seemed to have fooled an entire town with his generosity. He might not be a killer, but he wasn't a good man, like her father said. She pictured her great-grandad killing those people, and it made Kelcy feel a bit of shame. After all, they found him innocent, and there are no records to argue otherwise. You can't condemn a man for being strange. She tried not to envision his frail hands holding the bloody knife. The steam rising from the entrails splattered on the ice. Returning home after the trial, pleased he got away with what others did not. Is it the reason he smiled that way in the pictures? Because no one could have stopped him? Guilt rose in her chest and she cursed her mind for giving the gossip a place to fester.

Kelcy entered the dirt road and looked right to left, scanning its length. The lake was quiet, its silence screaming across the void as the intrusive thoughts poured forward. What if Becky couldn't keep her son safe? They were in the middle of nowhere, with nothing but a landline phone. All of this was nonsense. Fear brought on by her negativity. She needed to be stronger for her son. Not this. Kelcy shook off the negativity and scanned the woods, climbing the left side embankment. It created a barrier between her and the formidable depths. Kelcy felt trapped and her anxiety spiked, causing her balance to wobble out of sync. She stopped and turned, sensing the urge to run back into the cabin, pull Seth into her arms, and drift into the smell of his hair. She would thank Becky for the opportunity of self-reflection and then carry on with their day as if nothing happened. Forget about the lake and her great-grandad. Focus on more necessary things other than folklore. But that would not happen. Something held her within the story. It dug at the back of her neck, causing an itch to form. There was information missing. Facts mixing with folklore. That day with the tourists. How had the bodies become submerged under the lake's mouth? What Josephus had said when they had found him sitting with his legs in the fishing hole.

She took them, he said. *Who the fuck was she?*

Kelcy climbed back down and rounded the bend, looking back as her driveway disappeared from view. *They are fine. Seth is safe.* Hushing sounds of the water slapped the shore to her right, filling the gaps of threatening silence. The woods became denser. Shadows ebbed between pines, as strange cracks from the depths of its void whispered warnings. The intrusive thoughts returned. Kelcy shook her head, mumbling to herself to keep going. She ran the details over and over as she continued along the road. Three men came onto the ice that day and found Josephus sitting by a hole, feet submerged in the water. The severed head, missing its eyes and tongue. The victims were hooked to stringers. Why? He owned a fishery, and she supposed he had a good understanding of the lake. When he took those vacationers out that day, how did he not notice something was wrong on the ice? Was the storm that bad? If so, why the fuck did he bring those people out there? Maybe she was overthinking the entire thing. It is quite possible there was someone else with them on the ice. He was a known addict, not a liar. But then again, so was Bradley. She felt her cheeks flush at the thought.

There was a loud crack from the woods behind her left ear, and Kelcy spun around, raising her hands in alarm. Another crack sounded from deeper within the shadows, and her heart hammered in her chest. Her legs shuffled her forward against her will as she stared into the abyss, her eyes widening and drying at the edges. Tears streamed down her cheeks as the air between the pines cycled into a repeating whisper, "tooooookkk theeeeemmm." She locked her knees and tried to turn her head as a rumbling sound vibrated under her feet. "sheeeee-toook-thhh-emmm." Her leg jerked back, and the skidding of tires choked the voices. Kelcy put her hand to her chest and twisted her head. A man stared at her wide-eyed from under the brim of a baseball cap. The engine of the pickup truck sputtered as he jerked the gear into park. He tilted his head as he leaned out the window. As the man hopped out of his pickup, Kelcy wiped her face with the sleeve of her jacket. The stranger propped his hands on his waist.

"Kelcy?" He removed his hat and gave her a warm smile.

"Now I didn't expect to see you back here!" he clapped his hands together and approached her, holding out his arms. Kelcy took a step back and extended her hands in protest. The young man stopped in his tracks, letting his arms drop to his sides. "You forgot me that quick, huh?" He squeezed the brim of his hat, pulling off his head and slapping it against his outer right thigh, giving her a disappointed glare. She stared at his face for a moment and then covered her mouth and bent her knees.

"Christopher?" She placed her hand on her belly and took a deep breath to steady her nerves.

"Yea, but just Chris." He chuckled.

Kelcy rushed towards him and wrapped her arms around his neck, squeezing him into a bear hug. Chris let out a grunt and hugged her back. "Well, shit." He laughed.

She pulled away in relief and looked him up and down. Chris tucked his hat back on his head and leaned against the hood of his truck.

"What are you doing here, besides trying to get run over?" He tucked his other hand in his pocket and raised his eyebrows, waiting for an explanation. Kelcy folded her arms across her chest and looked toward the woods.

"Did you see anything when you were coming down the road?" She asked.

Chris looked into the woods and flattened his expression. "I wasn't really paying attention," he shrugged. "There was this girl with a death wish and I..."

Kelcy smirked and reached across, giving him a shove. "I'm serious." Her face tightened. Chris cleared his throat and looked at his feet. "Nah." he looked out toward the treeline. "What exactly happened?" he asked. Kelcy stared out over the lake, turning her back to the trees.

"Didn't see anything, just heard." She paused, squaring her chest. "Heard a loud snap, like footsteps." She looked at her feet.

Chris yanked on the brim of his hat and thought for a moment. "Could've been a bear?" he offered, rolling his fingers on the hood of his truck. She nodded, watching the shoreline. "Could've." She agreed.

"So." he kept drumming his fingers until Kelcy gave him a stern look. He retracted his hand and cleared his throat again, straightening his posture. "You at the old cabin?" he looked at the top of his boots.

"Yea?" Kelcy kept her gaze on the lake. Chris smiled and turned up the right side of his face. "Mom and Dad wanted me to come and stay for a while," she rolled her eyes. "Some solitude." She added before Chris interjected. He turned down the corners of his mouth and blinked, exaggerating the emotion.

"Ahh, solitude?" he shook his head. Kelcy looked over and squinted, letting him know she didn't appreciate the sarcasm or the gesture.

"Yes." She looked back out toward the lake. "Going through some rough times."

Chris nodded and gave the hood of his truck three loud slaps. "Well, let's get you back home," he smiled. "Before whatever it is you heard comes back."

He looked out towards the woods. He circled the cab and opened the passenger side door, gesturing for her to climb in. "Wouldn't want you to get hit by a truck." He added, his smile manifesting into an evil grin. Kelcy stood in defiance, trying to think of a witty way to tell him to fuck off. When he tilted his head and looked toward the cab, she gave up and climbed in, folding her arms across her chest to let him know she still wasn't pleased about his comments. He bowed his head and pinched the brim of his ball cap before circling the cab and climbing into the driver's seat. Without another word, he started the truck and headed off down the road. Kelcy looked over her shoulder at the passing trees. The anxiety in her chest eased as the bend faded behind them. "I'll turn around up ahead." He twisted the knob on the radio. Soft jazz filled the cab, and Kelcy looked over at him with wide eyes. "What?" he raised his left eyebrow. "You didn't take me for a jazz kinda guy?"

Chapter 8: Fast Friends

Christopher Hume, a twelve-year-old snob who lived across the lake, walked around with his iPod stuffed in his back pocket, singing pop tracks out of tune. Kelcy never spoke to him in passing, and he ignored her existence. His older brother Mark, who everyone called Fester because of his bald head, ran a small lawn mowing business. Christopher worked weekends, clipping hedges and mowing lawns for customers without pretty daughters. One day, Mark was mowing lawns, and a few days later day; he vanished. Kelcy wondered how someone could just disappear. Rumors started to circle the town that he knocked up some underage girl and when her father found out, he reported it to the authorities. Mark skipped town. The other rumor involved him going to jail, but it would have been in the local papers, so Kelcy added the rumor to the bullshit gossip category.

Hey, Christopher!" she yelled down the hill. Her voice echoed across the lawn and he kept walking as if he didn't hear her. She scowled and sucked the straw in her glass of iced tea. If he was being an asshole, he could keep on walking. Kelcy rolled her eyes and placed the glass at her feet. Cupping her hands around her mouth, she took a deep breath in. "Christopher!" She bellowed, holding the end of his name until her breath ran out. He stopped and looked up at the porch with his hands tucked in his pockets. She looked down the hill at him and turned the corner of her mouth up. She thought he looked pathetic, walking all slumped over. Kelcy signaled him to come up, and he stood there staring as if he wasn't sure he wanted to. He was pissing her off, and she cupped her hands again, taking a deeper breath. She stopped as her lungs expanded to full capacity and then gave him a wave of dismissal. Christopher scratched his head and started walking up the drive. Kelcy watched in amazement as he broke into a light jog, ascending the hill like an all-star athlete. He stopped at the bottom of her porch, putting his hands on his knees, bending forward, his chest heaving.

"What's up?" he huffed, peering at her from under the tuft of hair that covered the right side of his face. He spit on the ground and stood upright, placing his hands on his hips and stretching his puny chest. Kelcy tried not to laugh. She bent over, picked up her glass, and leaned back in her seat.

"Want some?" She took a big sip and puffed out her cheeks. Chris wiped his mouth with the back of his hand and then climbed the porch steps. "Sure." He plopped down in the chair next to Kelcy. She watched his chest rise and drop, waiting for him to pass out. As his breathing regulated, Kelcy got up and headed inside, returning with his glass of iced tea. She handed it to him and then slouched in her chair, sipping from her refilled cup. Using her thumb, she wiped the sweat from her glass and studied the mark. "Heard what happened to your brother." She said, as a matter of fact, wondering if she sounded heartless.

"It's fucked up." Christopher groaned, and Kelcy gave him a serious look, opening her eyes wide and puckering her lips. "Shhhh, watch your mouth, idiot. My parents are right inside." She warned.

"Sorry," Christopher bowed his head, looking out toward the lake.

"I'm sorry about Mark." Kelcy lowered her voice, taking a shot at sympathy. Chris didn't bite and took a swig of his drink. He looked over at her out of the corner of his eye. "His choice." He mumbled.

"Right." Kelcy smiled. She could tell he didn't mean it.

Chris took another huge gulp of iced tea and nodded his head. A smile creased her mouth as she relaxed in her chair. She wanted to ask him. Come out with it. But she needed to be careful.

"None of the rumors are true, you know," Chris said, resting the glass on his knee. Kelcy dropped her jaw and stuttered for words. He beat her to it, spoiling the chance to use subtle tactics, so she played dumb and shook her head. Chris gave her a hard stare. "Don't act like you haven't heard them, Kelcy."

He had said her name. She looked away, bobbing her head around, not knowing how to respond. Of course, he knew it. How the hell would he have not? He mowed their lawn for several summers, for Christ's sake. Her father called these types of things Small Town Saturday Night. She didn't understand why he chose that phrase, but he would stare down at her and add, "This world is a small place, Kelcy." Then why not say that? He loved to reference his favorite song titles, especially Hal Ketchum songs. He was weird like that sometimes. Maybe he was weird all the time. Christopher played with the rim of his glass as Kelcy thought about whether they should end the conversation. Christopher guided her once again with the inside information.

"Mark was last seen at Deacon Ballaster's house." He said, studying the rim of his glass.

Kelcy sat forward and tilted her head, wondering where he was going with the information. She coaxed him along, repeating the name. "Deacon Ballaster?" She squinted her eyes. Christopher took another sip of his iced tea and shook his head. "Well," she cleared her throat, resting her elbows on her knees, and dangling the glass between her legs. "I have two questions." He eyed her with suspicion and let her continue. "One, how do you know that, and Two," she closed one eye as if she was trying to process her thoughts. "What does that have to do with his disappearance?" Chris nodded and leaned back in his chair and took a deep breath. Kelcy got ready for the spilling of the beans and he didn't disappoint.

"I overheard the police talking to my mom." He paused and tapped the rim of his glass with his forefinger. Kelcy thought about her secret missions and realized he would have made a superb partner. He harbored some great eavesdropping skills.

"They found his truck down by the lake, a receipt for a soda on the front seat." He eyed her. "And a handwritten note from Mr. Ballaster saying he wasn't paying him for the shit job he did on their hedges." Kelcy looked at the door and Chris apologized again before continuing. "There was no girl, or pregnancy, or any of that sh..crap." He corrected himself. Kelcy felt completely lost.

"What?" She squinted her eyes. "So, he just bought a soda, parked his truck down by the water, and walked off into the sunset?" Her bottom jaw lay slack as her eyes drooped. "So what are you saying happened?" She straightened her face.

Christopher looked at her and shrugged. "Personally," he frowned. "All that nonsense about a note." He shook his head. "I think it was placed." Kelcy nodded her head and stared wide-eyed at the floorboards, trying to connect what he was saying. "I think someone killed him." He said, filling in the blanks.

Kelcy almost dropped her glass. She looked back toward the porch door that led to the kitchen, not sure if either of her parents were still in there. She turned to Chris and lowered her voice. "You think?" She placed her hand on his knee and then jerked it away, feeling her face flush. Chris gave her a serious nod and looked up. His eyes widened as if he was staring at a ghost. Kelcy continued, ignoring his expression. "You got any proof?" She whispered. His face grew pale as Kelcy followed his gaze to the porch window above her right shoulder. Fear trickled her spine as her heart slammed against her chest. Her dad stood at the window, smiling down at them.

"Christopher," he leaned on the windowsill. "How are you doing, son? Sorry to hear about your brother." Christopher nodded and looked down at his glass. "I know you're going through a hard time, but you have to be careful with wild accusations like that, son." Kelcy's father looked over at her and smiled. "Small Town Saturday Night, you know what I mean?"

Chapter 9: Small Town Saturday Night

They pulled up the drive as Becky walked out with Seth wrapped around her waist. Stepping onto the porch, she eyed the truck with suspicion. Kelcy stepped out, and Becky averted her eyes towards Chris, raising her eyebrows and smiling like a giddy child. Kelcy shook her head and walked up the steps, using her right arm to assist her forward. Chris followed behind, keeping his eyes on his feet. Becky met them at the edge of the porch, handing off Seth when Kelcy reached out.

"Who's your friend?" She winked.

"I'm Chris." He offered before Kelcy had time to introduce him. He pinched his hat and gave Becky a wide grin. She looked over at Kelcy, tilted her head, and widened her eyes. "I'm a childhood friend of Kelcy's." He leaned against the railing of the porch, grinning ear to ear.

"Well, nice to meet you, Chris." Becky nodded. "I'm the nanny." She looked around the porch and then pointed at Kelcy. "I forgot I have to stop at the grocery store!" She gave Kelcy a surprised look, trying to keep herself from smiling like a fool. "Is it okay if I leave a little early today?" Kelcy opened her mouth to answer as Becky leaned in, pecking Seth on the cheek before going inside to get her jacket and purse. Becky walked back out and nodded at Chris, then turned to Kelcy and winked. "Thanks." She hopped down the steps. "It was nice meeting you, Chris." She yelled, waving her hand above her head. Becky bounced down the driveway to her car.

"Same." He chuckled and looked over at Kelcy with an exhausted look. "Is she always weird like that?" He watched Becky pull away and head down the drive a little faster than she needed to. Kelcy hugged her son and kissed his head before setting him down. "He's yours!" The surprise in his voice made her uneasy, and she stared at Chris as Seth waddled back inside. Anxiety climbed up her back, and she twisted her mouth, folding her arms across her chest. The anxiety turned into defense.

"Yes, he sure is," she said with a tinge of sarcasm.

Kelcy looked into the kitchen to make sure he wasn't getting into any trouble. "His name is Seth." She put on a faux smile, nodding toward the door for them to go inside. He took the hint and followed her into the kitchen. Chris stood in the small room and tucked his hands in his pockets. He wasn't sure the kitchen looked as he had remembered it and scanned the room, trying to jog his memory. He heard nothing about her having a child, and he didn't remember Kelcy being the kind that would want one. Then again, few people around here talked about their family outside of the traditional gossip. They were still young when they last saw each other, and things have a way of changing. People change. Children made Chris nervous, and he tried not to be around them often. He was never sure how to act with kids, which created a tension that he had no control over. He hated that feeling. Pulling a chair, Chris sat at the kitchen table, as Seth climbed up into a seat across from him. The boy grabbed a handful of blocks, his body jerking from the loud clunk as he slapped them against one another. Chris observed the spectacle, raising his eyebrows and solidifying why he didn't want children of his own.

"You want a snack before nap time, Peapod?" Kelcy called over her shoulder as she washed her hands. Seth slapped the bricks together and shook his head no. Chris considered the transaction and doubled down on his opinion. Parenting is not for him. Too many variables. The responsibility would overwhelm him. He would never say his opinions out loud, especially around Kelcy, but he considered children to be a curse. They were supposed to survive you, fulfill your life, not remind you of your limited vitality. If something happened and your child passed away, you were stuck with something worse. He imagined there could be nothing worse than losing a child, and that was one of many things on the growing list of reasons he didn't want one.

"Would you like some water?" Kelcy interrupted his thoughts.

Chris pushed the negative opinions toward the pit of his stomach and smiled at Seth. He wanted her to believe he was better than his beliefs. "Sure." He turned his gaze up and pulled off his hat, placing it over his knee. She pulled a glass from the cupboard and ran the faucet for a second before filling it and placing it in front of him. He watched as the sediments swirled, making their way to the bottom of the glass.

"Sorry, I don't have a Brita or something." She picked up Seth, placed his bricks on the table, and headed toward the living room. "I'll be back. I am putting him down for his nap." Chris shook his head and took in the room again.

"I've been here my whole life, Kelcy." He mumbled. "I have drank my fair share of lake water." He took a sip as she disappeared into the depths of the house. "My whole life," he whispered to himself, placing the cup on the table. A small puddle formed under his cup as he twisted in his chair to look at the space behind him. The last time he spent time in the cabin, she was preparing to return home for her senior year. She never came back. They had kissed that summer, and for a while, he had blamed himself for never seeing her again. His stupid decision had pushed her away, or at least he assumed he did, and over time, he learned to bottle his emotions. Shove it down. Just like his feelings about his brother. She was crossing one of the biggest milestones in a teenager's life. Her path was about to change for the better, and he would not be part of it, and in some odd way, he had been okay with it. Chris tapped the table and looked across the room down the hallway that opened to the east side of the cabin. He stood up, placing his hat on the table before crossing the room and pausing at the entrance. The dark corridor led to Kelcy's bedroom and looked ominous. The bottom of her door leaked natural light onto the hardwood floor of the hall and he closed his eyes. Chris envisioned her lying on the bed, arms draped over her chest. Her eyelids glowed in a soft shade of pink as her lips pushed into a pout.

"You ok?" Kelcy's voice shot across the kitchen. Chris spun around, clearing his throat, and Kelcy gave him a smirk as he slumped his shoulders. He stepped back toward the center of the room and laughed, placing his hand on his chest while shaking his other finger. "You scared the b-Jesus out of me." He looked back toward the hallway and noticed the faded squares peppering the wall, disappearing into the depth of the corridor.

"You took down the old pictures!" He realized, staring back at her in amazement.

Kelcy held a placid expression. "Nope, they were gone when I got here." She pulled a chair, sitting and crossing her legs. "Actually," she tapped the table with the side of her thumb. "All the family pictures are gone." She shrugged her shoulders. He looked at the faded wallpaper and sat down in his chair, leaning back and taking a sip of water. A solid puddle formed under his glass, and he reached over, grabbed a napkin from the middle of the table, and wiped up the circle of water. He gave her an apologetic look, and Kelcy dismissed it with a wave. The more he looked around the room, the more he realized that nothing here was as he remembered it. Too many years have passed. Time has a way of fading things. He wondered when the memories of his brother would fade. He took two more mouthfuls and set the glass down with a solid clank.

"So," he smiled. "Why are you really back?"

The question surprised her. Its sudden delivery came off a little harsh and accusing. She stared at the table and gathered her thoughts. She could tell him to fuck right off, but that would get her nowhere. It's just a conversation. She was being over-sensitive. So, what did he need to know?

"My parents gave me the house." She lied. He stared at her in disbelief. She went to repeat herself and he tilted his head, interrupting her.

"To own? Like, you live here permanently now?" He squinted one eye.

She heard the doubt in his voice and wanted to slap him. Her eyes twitched. Was he calling her a liar? The irony made heat climb up her face, and Kelcy folded her arms around her stomach and sulked. She needed to stop being defensive if she was expecting him to stick around. Was she? *Tell him the truth, Kelcy.* The real reason her parents had sent her out here. Mental instability. A failed marriage. The inability to support her child. Just blurt it all out. Confess. If anyone would understand besides Becky, it might be him. She remembered the look on his face that summer. He understood loss. But under that pain, Chris harbored a kindness, but she needed to be careful. Kelcy nodded. Tightening her face.

"Yeah, to like, live in." She lied again. They stared in silence. A grin bent his face upward, and Kelcy dropped her defiance and raised her arms across her chest. She shook her head in disbelief. He hadn't changed at all. She rolled her eyes as he gloated. He was fucking with her.

"Well, shit," Chris burst into laughter, slapping the table with his palm. "I would have never thought you would move back to Cossayuna Lake."

She lifted her hands, shrugged her shoulders, and squinted out of the corner of her eyes. Chris chuckled as he spun his empty glass with his thumb and forefinger. Kelcy looked out towards the living room, his smile fading as he followed her gaze. He wanted to ask about the boy's father. There was shame in the question and he felt like a bastard asking her to confess what he already assumed.

"He got a dad?" The words floated rough and shaky from his mouth. Kelcy pursed her lips and rested her hands on the table. Sweat formed on her palms and Kelcy balled her fists.

"Yeah, of course he does." She watched her handprints fade into the worn tabletop. She couldn't talk about Bradley with him. Chris bit down on the guilt. Heat climbed up his neck as he leaned his elbows on the table and gripped the back of his head with both hands.

"I mean, like, is he?" he paused, waiting for her to stop him.

"In the picture?" She asked for him, closing her eyes as the words spilled from her mouth. "He died." The words held a finality, and now she wished for this moment to be a lie. She opened her eyes, averting them to the table, and steadied her breathing. Her anxiety swelled in her stomach, making her feel like she might throw up.

Chris sat back, slumping his hands in his lap. *Bad idea Chris. Asking that question.* He didn't need to know. It wasn't his business. If it had been a few minutes later. Finished his coffee before he climbed in his truck this morning. Just a few lousy minutes. The one time he didn't procrastinate. None of that mattered. Not in a place this small. This would have happened somehow, somewhere. As if she read his mind, Kelcy tapped the table with her right hand and stood up.

"It is what it is, Chris." She lied, easing his guilt. Now she was lying to herself. They left him there, in that house, to rot alone forever, running away back to her Mommy and Daddy. She took her son and left Bradley with nothing but a lonesome eternity, and someday, she knew, someone would return the favor. She stood over Chris, leaning on the table as he looked up at her with guilty eyes. He thumbed the rim of his glass and waited to be asked to leave. "Remember that day on the porch when we were kids, and you told me you think someone killed your brother?" She focused her eyes on his.

Chris felt his spine tighten. It's been a long time since he talked about Mark. Several years. The sound of his name coming from someone else's lips made his face hot. He couldn't imagine why she would drag up a conversation that took place between them when they were nothing more than crazy teenagers. Memories dug their way forward, replaying like the broken fragments of a record. Mark's truck. Abandoned by the lake. The newspaper clippings of him staring back from a high school photo. Kelcy's dad, behind the screen at the porch window, his face contorted in shadows. *What the hell did that man say that day? Something about a Saturday Night?*

"I don't talk about Mark," he snapped. The harsh tone of his response surprised him, and he cleared his throat as he straightened his posture. He would not discuss Mark with a girl he hadn't seen in over a decade. But yet, he expected her to talk about her son's father. His ears became hot, and he took a steady breath. "I'm sorry. Can I have some more water, please?" He looked up and tried to keep his eye contact neutral. He wanted to stand up and tell her this wasn't going to solve anything. Tell her to forget about the past. But he had just pried her about Seth's father? Being a hypocrite wasn't a good look. For once, he didn't want to be *that guy*. He needed to know why she brought it up. A soft panic rose in his belly. Did she have information about Mark's disappearance? Chris placed his hands on the table as Kelcy took his glass, refilled it, and placed it on the table in front of him. When she backed away, her hands were shaking and guilt punctured a hole straight through his chest. He let out a long moan and steadied his voice. The delivery needed to be in a calm tone. He needed to quell the growing anger. "What is going on, Kelcy?" He asked, pulling the glass of water closer, and focusing on the sediment. She studied his face, contemplating how she would deliver the punch. The punch was, to say the least, a stretch, but if anyone was going to listen to her, she believed it was Chris.

"So, I need you to listen." She sat, making stern eye contact, waiting until he focused on her. When their eyes locked and she was sure she had his complete attention, Kelcy crossed her forearms and rested her weight on her elbows.

"What do you know about the folklore of this lake?" She asked, keeping her tone flat and serious. Chris narrowed his eyes into a squint and turned up a corner of his mouth.

"Don't fuck around with me, Kelcy, not after mentioning my brother. Seriously." The agitation in his voice matched his eyes, and Kelcy tried to approach it from a different angle.

"When you almost ran me over earlier, I." She continued.

"When you stepped out in front of my truck, you mean?" He interrupted and Kelcy closed her eyes and steadied herself. *Now is not the time to start a point-of-view argument, Kelcy.* She needed him to listen.

"When I stepped out, yes." She continued, pulling a smile, hoping that he didn't read the sarcasm on her face. "I heard something in the woods, that's why I didn't notice you there."

Chris nodded his head. "Yeah, an animal." He gave her a bored look. He took a deep breath and calmed himself as she squeezed her forearms and nodded.

"I am not so sure if that's what it was, Chris," she said.

Chris gave her a confused look, and took a drink of his water, wiping his mouth with the back of his hand. He looked off into the depths of the cabin. "Well," he puffed out his cheeks. "Could have been the neighbor. What the hell's his name?" He looked around above his head as if the name hovered there somewhere and he was about to pluck it. "Chet Caster." He shouted, making Kelcy jump and shake her head, satisfied with the recall.

"No, I don't think it was a person, Chris." she nodded her head.

His expression hardened. "Wait? What are you saying?" She looked down at her forearms, pulling her lips into a thin line. Realizing what she was getting at slapped Chris across the face. "You thinking it was a fucking sasquatch or some shit?" He raised his voice, then looked out toward the living room. Kelcy squeezed her arms when he gave her an irritated look and placed his glass down on the table. She hugged her chest and looked at the floor. Chris stood up and backed towards the door. He adjusted his hat as he mumbled to himself. "He was my brother, Kelcy. My fucking brother." His expression tightened as he spat the words through his teeth. He didn't want to wake the boy, and he clenched his jaw as he looked toward the living room again. "You know, I get being out here alone may be scary, and maybe you need time to adjust, but this, this shit." His hand shook as he extended his finger and pointed to the tabletop. "You're not dragging what happened to Mark into this town's superstitious nonsense." Fear gripped her by the throat. Seth slept, oblivious to the danger she may have put him in. Chris needed to leave. The old Chris didn't exist anymore. This person terrified her. Kelcy believed something lurked in those woods. It was studying her. Listening. When he almost ran her over, relief flooded over her. He had saved her from whatever the hell it was. But he was a stranger now. The person shaking in her kitchen was not the Chris she grew up with, and she had not been the Kelcy he kissed that summer for a long time. She needed Bradley. Why did she come here without him? Abandoning his soul to that shitty apartment. The selfishness made her face burn. She pushed down the memories of him as much as she could, but now, when they might be in danger, she wished for him. An act of self-preservation. Bradley would hate her if anything happened to Seth.

"You need to leave." She glared at him. Her shoulders trembled as Chris stood in the doorway with a lump growing in his throat. He wiped his mouth and tried to calm his breathing. Kelcy understood she had made him upset, but she couldn't have that here, around her son. This town swept his brother's disappearance under the rug and moved on as if he meant nothing. They all considered them troublemakers, justifying the rumors over the facts. Kelcy believed it was murder, not some teen love gone bad. Chris may not want to listen to her about weird sounds in the woods, but there had been something out there. It spoke to her. She heard it. He considered the only monsters to be the townsfolk. Chris looked at the floor and closed his eyes. Kelcy bent her head forward, resting her forehead against the table. Tears splashed on her pant legs as a soft breeze cooled her face. When she looked up, she was sitting in an empty kitchen with an open front door.

Chapter 10: Downward Spiral

Kelcy locked the door as Chris's truck snaked down the drive, kicking up dirt as he bounced onto the main road. She slept on and off that night, unable to shake her anxiety, tossing and turning in the darkness. She lay in bed, listening to Seth breathing in the other room, as the shadows on the ceiling played tricks. They contorted, creating creatures that swirled above her. Thoughts of packing necessities and just disappearing felt more like a goal than a fantasy. If they did, she wouldn't tell anyone. Not her parents, or her friends back home. Especially not Chris. *What fucking friends*, she thought, tears welling and blurring her vision. They would take clothes, important documents, like birth certificates and social security cards, the little money she had, and disappear. Everything else could rot. Maybe she would park their car outside of town, vanishing like Mark. It worked before, right? Kelcy's chest tightened. "I'm sorry, Chris." She had whispered into the darkness. He didn't deserve that.

Something nudged against her ribs and she popped her eyes open and looked down toward her belly. Seth lay curled up against her side, his arm over her abdomen. A tuft of dark hair obscured his face. She looked over at the analog clock and moaned. The light from her bedroom window leaked in and stabbed at her eyes. She draped her forearm over her face and let out a soft moan.

"You awake Peapod?" She whispered.

Seth squeezed and snuggled into her, pretending to still be asleep. Kelcy ran her fingers up and down his spine as he giggled, squirming and kicking his legs. She wouldn't uncover her face, afraid that the sun would burn her eyes out. Rolling to her side, Seth adjusted his position with her and looked up. The ache in her chest almost brought her to tears. They couldn't leave. They needed stability, and she needed to stop running. No matter how far away she went, he would always be there in her mind. Rotting in the home she left him in. Maybe she needed to go back to therapy? Kelcy rolled her eyes and looked down. His little mouth stretched into a smile as he tilted his head onto her chest. Her heartbeat thumped against his temple, and she hugged him hard enough to hurt him, relenting when he produced a squeal.

"Too hard, Mommy," he grunted under her chin.

She imagined him scrunching up his nose and piercing his eyes. The same face he would make whenever anything green hit his plate.

"Sorry, Peapod." She kissed the top of his head and relaxed her neck. This is how she wanted to stay. Suspended like this. Forever. If only. Fading to sleep and never awakening. Her stomach twisted, and she bit her tongue, cursing herself. Bradley would never want that for them. This was the second time in two days that she had dug him from the grave for selfish reasons. She knew how much of a lie it was. Bradley was always in the back of her mind. His name dug its way forward, and she wanted him to slither from the shadows and comfort them. She could never let him go. He was the father of their child. She loved him, and in his own twisted way, he had loved them. Never enough to stay, but he loved them. She opened her left eye and peered at her alarm clock again. Nine-fifteen. Becky would arrive in two hours and she needed to have Seth fed and ready. Kelcy slid out from under him and he pulled the covers over his head, giggling as she stood up. Kelcy stretched her arms toward the ceiling and stood in silence, watching Seth worming under the blanket. She circled, in a slow arch, around the other side of the bed with her hands out like claws. Just as he peeked out to where he thought she was standing, she snatched him up from behind, laughing like a witch. Seth yelped and broke into laughter as she pulled the sheets away, scooped him up, and set him on the floor, before squatting face level.

"Go get dressed, Peapod. Becky will be here soon." She ruffled his hair.

Seth smiled and nodded, and took off running, leaving Kelcy alone in her bedroom. This is how things are now. Alone. Without him. The sound of Seth pulling open drawers echoed from down the hall. The SpongeBob theme song twists off the walls, swirling his voice into something nefarious as anxiety gripped her spine, causing her to double over. Moments like this made the experience of loneliness manifest into madness. Sometimes, Seth made facial expressions that made him look like Bradley. Pronunciations emanating from his little mouth in the familiar tone that existed before his birth. Handed down by his father as a reminder of her choices. One day, she would lose her mind. Alone in her thoughts with what might have been. What she had walked away from. Kelcy rocked on the floor as visions of their old apartment haunted her. She cleaned the kitchen, as the laundry rattled in the dryer. The clicking sound of a random zipper snapping in a rhythmic sequence. Like the hands of a ticking bomb. He would be home soon. Fumbling through the door with his guitar cases. Leaning them against the wall and strolling up to her with that smile. She could smell the intoxication on his skin. The sickness. Her heart hurt for him. A high-pitched voice in the distance told the story of a man's flight toward the sun as they embraced. Guitars screamed as the rhythmic gallop moved their bodies in unison. He had made a promise. A forever that she knew had been a lie. And for a while, she wanted to believe him.

    Intimate moments with Seth were supposed to be for both of them. Did Seth understand he could never see his father? Did he have to hear that addiction ripped him away from them? When would he realize Bradley is not coming back? A sudden weight pulled on her shoulders. Her breath dragged from her lungs, threatening to suffocate her. Did he remember Bradley? Kelcy dry heaved as panic overtook her and tears made micro puddles on the floor. Seth appeared in the doorway dressed in a pair of play jeans and a Matchbox shirt. His mismatched socks, one blue, one green, wiggled out from under his pant legs. His face became concerned.

"What hurts Mommy?" He scrunched his nose. She turned her face away and wiped her eyes with her sleeve.

"Nothing Peapod, Mommy is fine." She scooped him up and made her way to the kitchen to get ready for Becky. "Toast?" She placed Seth in a chair and pulled a coffee mug from the rack next to the sink.

"Yup!" He shook his head, grabbing the salt and pepper shakers from the tray in the center of the table. They became imaginary aircraft, flying around the tabletop, their fuselage leaving speckles of white and black in their wake. He smacked them together and made an explosive sound as he giggled. Kelcy placed her mug under the Keurig and popped a dark roast K-cup into the top slot. She pressed the drip button and walked away to get the bread when Becky barged through the door.

"Well, good morning, you two!" She looked back and forth between them. Seth paused and waved at her, his grin matching the velocity of her excitement. Kelcy smiled, placing the bread in the toaster and fishing the peanut butter out of the cupboard. She could never understand how people had this type of energy in the morning. She would need to get up at two a.m. to power up like that. Becky hugged Kelcy's back and sat next to Seth.

"I have an idea!" She kneeled next to him. He kept on flying the shakers, oblivious to the conversation. Becky looked up at Kelcy from under her bangs. "How about I take you to the farmer's market this morning?" She made a large circle with her mouth. Seth clanked the shakers together and then looked over at Becky, a huge grin stretching across his face. "I take that as a yes?" She reached over and poked Seth in the top of his belly. He squirmed in his seat.

"Stop." He giggled.

"And what do you say, Mom?" Becky looked up at Kelcy with a Cheshire grin. Kelcy's heart skipped. After last night, she was unsure about leaving him with anyone. What if Chris came back for her, or saw them in town? Fear gripped her throat and squeezed. Was she exaggerating the situation? Chris might have been being an asshole, but he would never hurt them. Would he? Could Becky keep him safe? Kelcy knew she wouldn't let anything happen to Seth. She nodded against her will and took a sip of her coffee, while thoughts about how angry Chris had been when he left swirled in her head. Maybe they should leave this place after all. Bradley snaked his way forward again, slithering from the back of her mind. *Are you sure you want to go?* He hissed. If anything were to happen to Seth, Bradley would never forgive her. She would never forgive herself. Intrusive thoughts of Seth dying flashed in her mind's eye, and Kelcy's breath hitched. Would Seth also just become a voice? Something that she would leave behind? Her mind relayed visions of Seth wandering the halls of the cabin alone, and Kelcy panicked. Her hands shook and Becky stood up, her expression flattening with concern.

"It's ok Kelcy." She pulled her into a hug, and Kelcy relented. "What's going on?" She squeezed, pulling her back, and gripping her shoulders. Becky saw the fear twisted on her face and she pulled Kelcy back in as Seth continued to fly the shakers around the table. The toaster snapped, the loud clunk disrupting the silence. Kelcy pulled away and wiped her eyes, letting out an embarrassed laugh.

"Toast," she turned, grabbing the jar of peanut butter and unscrewing the lid. Becky went back to Seth and sat at the table, not sure how to proceed with the plans.

"How about we watch some cartoons instead?" Becky brightened her voice and looked at Seth for approval. Kelcy smeared the peanut butter through blurry eyes, placed the toast on a plate, and cut them into squares. Wiping her eyes again, she spun around and leaned over the table, sliding the plate in front of Seth. He dropped the shakers and snatched a square, smiling as he bit into the crust.

"No," Kelcy smiled. "Take him to the market."

Becky stared up and waited for her to change her mind, nodding and mouthing *okay* when Kelcy smiled at her, tears again welling in her eyes. "I will text you every five minutes if needed." She took out her cell and opened her contacts. Kelcy's throat clenched.

"I don't have a cell phone." She folded her arms and pressed her thumbnail between her two front teeth.

"What?" Becky placed the phone on the table and stared at Kelcy in astonishment. "No cell phone?" She said, her face contorting in confusion. The embarrassment climbed Kelcy's face, turning her cheeks a deep shade of red.

"I know, it's weird." She pulled a seat and sat down, yanking a napkin from the holder in the middle of the table and wiping her eyes. "I just never got another one after Bradley."

"OK, well," Becky pulled a smile and slid her phone back into her purse, clapping her hands. "We will call the house phone and leave a message if you don't answer!" She smiled down at Seth as if she were expecting him to make a note. Kelcy squeezed the napkin in her fist and watched Seth nibble at the edges of his toast. Peanut butter collected in the corners of his mouth, and his eyes widened as his jaw gaped open. He licked fervently and nodded his head. He looked manic. His eyes bulged like a death thing. The tongue jutted out like a worm, saliva-coated and sharp. Kelcy shook her head. A sickening feeling wormed in the pit of her stomach, and she closed her eyes.

"Ok," she turned and walked to the sink. Kelcy smiled and sipped her coffee. "You two have fun this morning. I may go for a walk." She went to Seth and kissed him on the top of his head, and then ruffled his hair. "You listen to Becky, ok?" Seth looked up and nodded.

"I'll be fine." She mouthed to Becky, pulling a smile as she raised the glass to her mouth.

"He will be ok," Becky mouthed back. "Promise."

"We should be back by one o'clock, two at the latest." She said out loud and turned to Seth, poking the top of his belly again. He giggled and squirmed in his seat, almost dropping his toast. They both let out a laugh, and Kelcy grinned.

"Ok." She wiped her face, trying to shake off the sickness that formed at the base of her gut. She could feel the corners of her mouth shaking. "Have fun and be safe." Kelcy looked down at Seth and Becky placed her hand on his back and gave her a serious look. There was an understanding between them. *I'll be fine. Keep him safe.* Kelcy translated. Two people who loved that little boy conversing through telepathy. But one had more to lose than the other, and Kelcy wouldn't let that be unknown between them. She gave Becky an unforgiving smile before heading back to her bedroom. She listened as Becky shuffled around the kitchen, getting Seth ready for their adventure. When the door slammed shut, Kelcy collapsed on her bed, grabbing the nearest pillow, squeezing it to her face, and screaming.

Chapter 11: Knock Knock

The end of her driveway cut into the road as the lake mirrored the dark clouds hovering over the cabin. They had been gone for a little over an hour, and Kelcy had emotionally bled herself. There was a shame in being a parent that those without children could never understand. The selfishness needed to let them go. The grip you would tighten when the fear of loss takes hold. But you will lose them. Year after year they climb into a chrysalis, reshaping into something else. A person you swear you recognize until they exhibit a foreign behavior, stealing your breath and reminding you that, soon, they will not be yours. In truth, they never were. In reality, you are a sentinel. Pouring yourself into their existence. Your love, your hopes, encased in the promise of forever, and in the end, you smile despite it. Parenting is a selfish occupation.

Kelcy stepped into the road and looked left, then right down the long stretch that curved along each side of the lake. Somewhere, on the opposite side, the gravel leads to the blacktop. Away from here. Kelcy knew of another world away from the lake. A place just as dark, and part of her questioned which place had the sharpest teeth. Right now, she wanted to hear Chris's truck kick the dust around the bend, speeding along the stones. Slamming to a stop at the entrance to her drive. Pinching his hat, and smiling at her. She needed someone. She fucked that up for sure, and there was a strong possibility she may never see him again. He did not deserve the thoughts she was having about him, and the shame made her feel sick. Kelcy headed down the dirt road in the opposite direction she had the other day. Closing her eyes, Kelcy walked as far as her inner senses would let her. Before fear made her open them, correcting her gate back to the middle of the road. She would close them again and concentrate, trying to stay towards the center. There were clicks and snaps from the woods to her left mixed with slaps and hushing of the shoreline to her right. Concentrating on each sound, Kelcy assumed their origin and tried to connect with it. She needed to know what was out there watching her. As much as she wanted to deny it, there was a connection to the lake as well. Four generations, her father had said. She could feel its energy seep from the trees. The hiss of the waves as they hugged the shoreline, melting everything into one huge aura.

    Kelcy had fond memories of the lake as a child. The innocence of not knowing the secrets within things. At nine years old, the next-door neighbor, an old native man named Robert, sat by the edge of the road. She spied on him every day during her secret missions from behind the large pine that guarded his property line. He spent hours looking out over the lake, eating hard candy, and rocking in his old metal chair. He looked ancient. Small divots and holes covered his face, giving his leathery skin a worn appearance. She would walk by, slowing her pace as she passed his driveway, waiting for him to acknowledge her. Kelcy would try to stifle her grin when he waved, letting out a whistle from between his teeth. He would share his candy while he told her stories about the lake. The townsfolk called it folklore, but Robert said some of it was history. Kelcy didn't understand it back then, but those tales came from his living diary. Stories passed down through generations. He was passing them to her as his family did years before him. She wondered if they might also be confessions. Of what, she wasn't sure, but there was a sense of guilt sometimes when she looked into his dark orb-like eyes. When she would retell them, trying to remember every detail, her father would smile, calling Robert a crazy old angler. "Take his tales with a grain of salt, kiddo. It's old Native mumbo jumbo." Her dad warned, picking at his plate. Her mother would nod along with nothing to add, playing along with whatever her father had to say.

She stopped at the foot of the drive and followed the winding path up to his cabin, now hidden by overgrown brush. She closed her eyes and relaxed her shoulders. Robert's voice whispered between the pines, rushing through the landscape and cascading over the surface of the lake. In her mind, she became nine again. Sitting next to him as he rocked in his brittle metal chair, staring out toward the lake. His voice was soft and sharp. The eyes, set deep in his weathered face, ebbed with the white teeth of the waves.

"Cossayuna is not the name of the lake." He smiled. "It is a mispronunciation of its native name, Quabbaunna." Kelcy sucked on the fruit-flavored candy, listening as if nothing else around them existed. "It means, The Lake of Three Pines." He continued, staring down at her with his beautiful black orbs. "My ancestors were Horican, but they are gone now." Kelcy's tongue, swollen with sugar, burned the roof of her mouth as she looked out over the lake. She imagined phantom images of his ancestors walking along the beach. "They were kin to the Mohican." He continued, looming over her. His features danced in the shadows of her peripheral vision. He reached over, patting the top of her hand. "Do you know of the Mohican?" She nodded her head and smiled. In school, her history teacher told them a story about them. A book they said she hadn't been old enough to read. She told her dad that she thought the teacher was stupid, and that she had been plenty old enough to read it. Her dad disagreed, and Kelcy called him an idiot under her breath.

"Yes!" She grinned between slurps of sugar.

The story talked about a mighty warrior named Uncas. She recalled, not sure of the pronunciation, and Robert nodded his head.

"A fictional story, yes," he eyed the water, grinning, "but a real Sachem." Kelcy gave him an odd look, and he explained Sachems were chiefs among the Algonquins from the North. He pointed toward the mountains. Kelcy remembered how serious he became when he spoke of his ancestors and the different inhabitants of the lake. He had told the stories as if they were all gone, as if he were the last, like Uncas. Her heart ached as she held back tears, struggling to listen about his family and their loss. In between the historical details, Robert weaved wild stories of supernatural things. Creatures and spirits that walked within shadows and spoke in foreign tongues, cursing some and guiding others. He told her about the powers of the lake. Kelcy's chest would pound as he came to the climax of every tale, pointing out over the water. He would stare down at her and lean in close. His breath, sweetened from the candy, filled her nose as he waved his hand out toward the horizon.

"Listen to the lake. It will talk to you. It can tell you things. Even warn you of things."

She looked into his deep eyes, memorized by his magic words. "What you give to it, it will return," He glared at her. "Remember that," he emphasized, his mouth turned down, elongating his features. "Never focus on what was taken or what has become lost. It will keep those. Only what you give to it will it return." Kelcy didn't repeat any of that to her parents. Especially her father. That was to stay between them. She would lie in bed at night, staring at the shadows on her ceiling as they twisted and danced. Imaginary creatures climbed the walls as the pines groaned outside her window. Her heart would thump in her ears like a great war drum until her eyes grew too heavy to stay awake. *What you give to it, it will return. Listen, it can talk to you.*

Kelcy stared up the drive to get a better look at Robert's old cabin nestled atop the hill. She was hoping someone had bought the old place. The thought of it being abandoned made her chest heavy. She remembered the day Robert had passed. There was an ambulance in his drive, and her dad told her to stay away. Kelcy had snuck out the back door and cut through the woods, being careful not to get caught. She refused to turn back, the image of her father traipsing through the woods to snatch her up, dragging her back home, grounding her to her room forever. Or at least the rest of the summer, which would feel like an eternity. She needed to see him. Hiding behind the huge pine at the edge of his property, Kelcy watched two men exit the front door. She gripped the tree, digging in with her nails, as tears welled, blurring her vision. The distorted image of a large white mass on a wheeled bed bumped down the stairs toward the back of the flashing emergency vehicle. Kelcy turned and ran, her chest heaving as she fought the urge to scream out. Her face burned as she wiped the tears and snot from her maw. Robert was gone. Her only genuine friend in this hellish place. She leaned against the back of her house and looked out over the lake. *It can talk to you, remember that.* Robert's voice floated up through the ether. She closed her eyes and pressed her back against the cold wood of the cabin.

Taking a few steps up Robert's drive, Kelcy paused and perked her ears. She inspected the exterior of the structure as best she could from her position halfway up the drive. It looked as if no one had lived there in several years. Patches of dense moss, dark green and black, had formed on the side of its walls, filling in the windows on the east side. Kelcy backed down into the road and sighed. Investigating further would have been useless. The cabin was in ruins, and its tall pine peeked at her above the treeline on the west end of his lot. She thought about the Quabbaunna. The three pines. It swayed over her, bending in consolation. Kelcy nodded and turned, leaving the haunted grounds to the sentinel. She looked out over the lake and frowned.

"I'm listening." She whispered.

Its reflection of the sky looked black and rotten and goosebumps ran down her arms as Kelcy studied its surface. Manipulating the beauty above and twisting the space between. The world in which we inhabit with minimal thoughts of what lies beneath. Places like this were supposed to be serene and clean, where you could escape the real dangers of the world. Its decayed depths hid its purpose under a crystalline mirror. The place was a fucking curse. The old man wasn't telling her, he was warning her. *It can tell you things.*

The road came to a bend. The trees to the right of the road hung over, creating ominous stark shadows across the gravel. Sparse groups of brush to the left cut the light into arrows, illuminating the ground in stripes. Kelcy paused and looked back toward her cabin. She would need to get back before they returned. She knew Becky had been more than capable of getting Seth a snack and laying him down, but that was her job. Her job was to be a mom. The one with the privilege of doing those things. Not a nanny.

After she passed the bend, the road straightened out, seeming to stretch on forever. Kelcy sighed and decided she didn't have the time or curiosity to explore today. A small trail cut into the woods, winding down to the shore. She contemplated going to the water's edge. To Listen. Robert's stories fought against her fears as her anxiety reared its ugly head. "It's just a lake." She assured herself. The old stories are metaphorical, most times, and she had been a nine-year-old girl when he filled her head with the mystical folklore. What nightmarish details did her imagination add over the years? Still, there is something to be said about intuition, and her gut ached whenever she got near that water. Guilt rose like a thunderstorm. Did she abandon Bradley for this? *Was this worth the free ride, Kelcy?* She could try to convince herself that the move improved the life of her and her son, but in reality, it was a weakness. It was better than to believe what the real purpose had been. The need to move on.

Oh, don't fool yourself. Her inner voice mocked.

"No, Seth needed security. I needed help." She talked to the trees.

So you believe Daddy offered this place up so you had financial security?

"Yes. I was broke. We were in trouble and this place has been empty for years, I..."

You sure? Or is this another means to control you? To control what happens to Seth? Daddy always hated Bradley. How are you going to move on from that?

"I know they didn't get along, but I don't believe Dad wanted anything to happen to him." Her head jerked around, scanning the woods for the voices' origin. Her head throbbed. "He said he was sorry for what happened to Bradley."

But, was he? A different, much deeper voice let out an echoing laugh from somewhere behind her. It cascaded across the lake's surface, disappearing into the void. Fear climbed up her neck, trying to strangle her. What was happening? A sense of madness pulled at her reality. Kelcy could feel her body separate from her mind.

"Bradley?" she called out. Did he dig his way from the recesses of her psyche? Ready to drag her to hell where she belonged. Kelcy pressed her palms against her temples and closed her eyes tight. She shook her head, trying to dislodge the voice. "Please don't do this to me." She whimpered.

Who are you going to trust? The voice slithered behind her eyes, and Kelcy squeezed her head tighter, gripping her hair in her fist. *The voice of reason, which with all due respect, is just you talking to yourself. Or the man who manipulated you into thinking he is a charitable Daddy who just wants the best for his little girl and grandson? Besides,* the voice gripped her brain and forced her eyes open, memories flooding forward. *You forgot about what his grandfather did to that little Russian girl. Your great-granddaddy was a wicked man.* Opening and closing her mouth like a fish, Kelcy's body shook. Her teeth gnashed together as images flooded her cerebral cortex. *Oh,* the voice hissed. *You had blocked that out?* Her throat clenched, and she gagged on the bile that rose from her stomach. *Check the basement and backyard for the Butter-Nut cans.* Kelcy's legs buckled, and she fell to her knees and expelled herself onto the road. *Coffee as sweet as a nut,* the voice laughed as she spilled the rest of her stomach contents onto the dirt. The smell of bile made her gag and Kelcy covered her mouth with the back of her hand as she dry heaved. The voice faded, and she sat up panting. Vomit dribbled from her bottom lip as she placed her right hand on her knee and pushed herself up. She looked over the lake as her mind caught up with her senses. She needed to get back to the cabin. Kelcy broke into a staggered run. She needed to get Seth and Becky away from this fucking lake.

Chapter 12: Stay for Dinner

Chris ran down the steps as Kelcy stumbled into the drive, slumped over with her arms dangling at her side.

"What in the hell happened?" He leaned up against her, draping her arm over his shoulder.

She looked up at him in confusion and let her head drop to the side. He hobbled her up the path and looked back to see if anyone or anything had followed her. Animal attacks, although rare in these parts, have happened in the past. Not over six years ago, close to here, a coyote dragged a young child off. They found his half-eaten body in the quarry at the other end of town. Maybe that's what she heard on the road that day. Chris inspected her for injuries as they climbed the steps to her porch. There were no tears in clothing or signs of blood anywhere, but the faint smell of vomit emanated from beneath her hair. Chris held his breath, trying to stifle his gag reflex. When he got her into the cabin, they walked to the living room. He laid her on the couch and stood staring over, watching her chest to make sure she was still breathing. This was not how his apology was supposed to go. He envisioned a cup of coffee mixed with several variations of, I was being a dick and I'm sorry. He pulled out his cell phone. Pecked 911 on the keypad, and stared at the top of his boots.

"911, what's your emergency?" The thin voice hissed through the receiver. He looked up to Kelcy, shaking her head in protest, and Chris furrowed his brow, pressing the phone to his ear.

"There's a woman here in need of medical help, and I..." He paused when Kelcy opened her eyes wider and shook her again. If he wanted her to give him a chance to fix what happened between them, this would not be a promising start. As much as he desired to continue, he clenched his teeth, cleared his throat, and said, "Sorry ma'am, false alarm." And hung up. Chris slipped his phone into his pants pocket and sighed. He held his hand up to speak and then cut himself off, looking at the floor in confusion.

"Thank you." She laid her head back, closing her eyes as she rubbed her temples. Chris nodded, gathering his thoughts. Her safety was the most important thing and his questions about the why and what the hell could wait.

"You want some water?" He asked, not waiting for her answer as he headed into the kitchen. He couldn't remember where she had kept the glass wear and started searching each cupboard. Chris ran through common explanations. Maybe one of those coyotes. Or one of those weirdos from up the hill? His anxiety spiked as his mind ran through images of her being attacked on the side of the road. He closed his eyes and centered himself. She seemed fine now, for the most part, and he was thankful, but he needed to know what happened. Maybe she has one of those diseases that causes seizures? His eyes lit up, and he hurried back into the living room, placing the glass on the end table next to her head. He crossed the room, sitting down in the armchair and leaning his elbows on his knees.

He needed to be careful in his wording. Keep the approach respectful. He focused on her, putting on an over-concerned expression.

"You got some kind of disorder or something?" He asked.

She opened her eyes and stared at him in disbelief. His face reddened with embarrassment and he bowed his head, cursing to himself. Kelcy inched her way up into a sitting position.

"Thank you." She grabbed the water, downing half the glass before placing it back on the table in a slow, careful motion. The clank made her scrunch her face up in pain. She pointed her finger at Chris and opened one eye. "No, I don't have some disorder or something." She drew out the first letter of the last word with a sarcastic hiss that made Chris lower his head deeper into his lap.

"I'm just trying to help." He mumbled from between his knees, and Kelcy took a deep breath as a pang of guilt stabbed at her chest. She didn't know the reason for his return, but lucky for her, here he sat, with his head in his lap. *So let's be an asshole, Kelcy.* She said to herself.

"I'm sorry Chris." She cupped her forehead, resting her elbow on the arm of the couch. Her brain pounded against the side of her skull, and she felt bile threatening to claw its way up and onto her beautiful wooden floor. She tightened her throat and tried to steady her nerves.

"It's okay." He made his lips into a thin line, looking up in concern. "I am glad I came over." He sat straight and focused his eyes. "By the way, the reason I came over was to.." She held up her hand, cutting him off and shaking her head realizing now what it is he came to do.

"We are even, for now." She forced a smile. Chris relaxed his shoulders and slumped back into the armchair. She was giving him a chance to fix things, and she didn't have to. Chris smiled and nodded. Kelcy thought he was an asshole, but there was no reason to think he would ever hurt them. He would need to earn that trust back. She raised an eyebrow.

"You're not free yet." She mocked, and Chris flattened his smile. Kelcy laughed, squinting in pain, and Chris let out an uncomfortable chuckle.

"Do you know anything about my great-grandad, Josephus?" She picked up the glass and studied his reaction over the rim. Chris stared into the void, his eyes searching the shadows in the room's corner. He pinched his eyebrows together and continued searching.

"I mean, besides the murders and all the gossip? Not a lot. Why?" He turned, rested his chin on his shoulder, and looked at her with a blank stare. Kelcy finished her glass of water and studied the rim.

"Just trying to piece things together." She closed her eyes and pinched the bridge of her nose.

"What things?" He leaned forward.

The front door burst open, and Kelcy squished her face up in a knot as Becky and Seth barged into the kitchen. The sound of bags ruffling and shoes scuffing the floor was like pins in her brain.

"Mommy!" Seth rushed in and jumped up onto the couch. Kelcy opened one eye and smiled. Becky walked in and froze, staring back and forth between Chris and Kelcy.

"Oh," she giggled, "I see you have company."

Kelcy twisted her mouth, giving her a comical scowl and Becky winked, causing Kelcy to roll her eyes. Chris smiled at Becky and straightened his posture as if he were going to say something. Kelcy gave him a stern look and shook her head. Whatever he was going to say, it could wait for another day. Chris looked at Kelcy out of the corner of his eye and smiled at Becky.

"Mommy!" Seth squeezed her face with his tiny, frozen hands, and Kelcy shivered. He pulled her stare to his and raised his eyebrows. "We saw a mewgichan!" Kelcy looked up at Becky, pretending to understand, nodding and smiling. Her brain was still foggy, but she didn't want to ruin his excitement.

"There was a musician at the market today." Becky laughed. Kelcy feigned surprise.

"Ahh." She pretended to pull an imaginary rabbit from the top of Seth's head. "A magician. Got it." She laughed. Chris smiled and went along as if Seth didn't annoy him with the entire spectacle. He would need to get over this kid thing if they were going to remain friends.

"Bought some stuff for dinner." Becky walked back into the kitchen and continued her conversation, yelling toward the living room. "Corn, veggie wraps, and hummus! You staying for dinner?" She popped her head around the corner and stared at Chris. He fumbled for an answer, looking at Kelcy for confirmation. "Awesome!" Becky smiled, answering for her, and then disappeared again, leaving Chris shrugging his shoulders and mouthing an apology. Kelcy smiled as Seth played with her hair.

"You smell bad, Mommy." Seth scrunched his nose. Kelcy set him down and looked over at Chris. "I'm gonna shower while you finish dinner." She yelled toward the kitchen, wincing.

"Coffee sounds wonderful, if you could?" She hovered, waiting for a response.

"You want some coffee too, Chris?" Becky yelled as the sound of running water echoed through the cabin.

"Sure," Chris called back and relaxed in his chair.

"Please watch, Seth?" Kelcy eyed him, her voice pounding in her temples. She hoped the caffeine would help with her headache. As she hugged her son, she stared at the doorway across the room leading to the basement. *You forgot about the Butter-Nut cans in the basement and backyard.* Kelcy closed her eyes and suppressed the voice. Chris didn't want to but nodded and smiled. If he could have run, he would have.

    They sat around the table as Becky shuffled back and forth, setting hot plates on top of folded hand towels. Chris sipped his coffee, raising his eyebrows while scanning each dish, acting as if he had an interest in what she had prepared. Kelcy had her hair up in a bun, sporting a pair of sweatpants and an old weathered hoodie with holes in the front pouch. Kelcy didn't have a healthy food type of personality. Her passions stayed within the pizza, chicken wings, and hoagies food pyramid. The greasier the better. Seth flew the salt and pepper shakers around, oblivious to the monstrosity he was about to be fed. Becky placed chicken nuggets and fries in front of him and Kelcy eyed him with a stab of jealousy. Seth dropped the shakers and clapped his hands, giggling as he grabbed a nugget and stuffed it in his mouth. Kelcy wanted to correct him, but her envy wouldn't allow it. She wanted to steal one, giving her friend the middle finger in protest. Becky sat at the table and grabbed a wrap, scooping up a heaping mound of hummus, smearing it, and then moving on to the next topping. Chris decided he might as well be the first victim, spreading a small dab of hummus onto a wrap. He made his way around each dish, scooping the smallest amount that wouldn't seem offensive. When he placed his wrap down, he looked at Kelcy and tried his hardest not to laugh. The apparent look of pain on her face somehow eluded Becky, and Chris was taking way too much joy in Kelcy's anguish. She pursed her lips as he tilted his head with a smile, picked up the wrap, folded it, and took a large bite. With a horrid grimace, he swallowed and took another, grinning at Kelcy, who was now on the verge of uncontrollable laughter.

"Okay." Becky looked at them, pretending to be disappointed. "I get it, you don't like it, but I worked hard on this, so be a pale and pretend k." She took a large bite and wiped hummus off the edge of her mouth with her index finger. Her eyes bulged when she swallowed, and Chris and Kelcy burst into laughter. Seth looked up with a fist full of fries and joined in, giggling as he stuffed his mouth.

"I worked hard on this for real." Becky put on a mock frown, and Kelcy gave her a serious look.

"Yeah, that hummus must have been hard to dump into a bowl," she scoffed.

"Fuck you," Becky laughed, covering her mouth and looking at Seth. Kelcy waved her hand as her son continued to play with his nuggets. Oblivious to the foul language.

"He has heard worse." She smiled, her face flattening.

He has, hasn't he? Bradley's voice crept up her spine. The memories of their argument flooded her mind. She was so pregnant with Seth that it looked like she had a basketball stuffed under her shirt. Kelcy held the bottom of her belly for support as she waddled around the apartment. She excluded him from dinner, at her father's request, and his anger spiraled out of control when she provided the excuse. He was leaving for a tour.

When she defended the decision, he yelled *fuck you and your family* and stormed from their apartment. She sat on the floor in the dark all night, holding her unborn child and crying until she almost threw up. They never spoke of it again.

She pulled a smile, fixing her wrap and taking a bite. Her face contorted, and Becky gave her a sour look. The table erupted into laughter again, and Kelcy wished she could, at least for a moment, have something else to concentrate on besides Bradley. Becky stuffed more in her mouth and then perked up, pointing through the screen door out towards the lake. Kelcy and Chris stared at the huge flecks of white orbs falling from the sky. Clouds hovered over the distant lake, heavy and black. Seth twisted a French fry between his fingers and pointed a fat chubby digit toward the falling orbs. His face lit up as he made a large oval with his mouth. He swung his feet, knocking his shoes together as he clamped his lips around the potato stick. The table sat in silence as the world climbed out from its chrysalis.

Seth swallowed and clapped his hands. "Snow Mommy!" He hooted.

Kelcy smiled and looked back out across the glass surface of the lake. Soon, it would freeze over and the anglers would come out. She wasn't sure if she was ready for the lake to be trapped under the ice. From her experiences, that's when it seemed to be the most vicious. Chris reached across and grabbed another wrap. Kelcy and Becky stared at him as he shrugged his shoulders, scooping a spoonful of hummus. He cupped the wrap in his hand and spread it across as the girls looked at each other in amazement. When Becky smirked, Chris paused, pulling his lips into a thin line, and eyed her with a look of sarcasm.

"What?" he scoffed, making his way around each bowl, creating a huge mound in his hand. Kelcy chuckled at him, and Chris raised one eyebrow. "First jazz, and now this? I can't like anything, I guess." Kelcy pursed her lips and raised her middle finger. Chris coughed and raised his hands. "There is a child here!" He pointed at her son and tilted his head with a look of disappointment on his face. Becky looked at them and leaned her arms against the table.

"You guys need a room?" She scanned their faces.

"NO!" they both shouted, staring at each other.

Becky rolled her eyes and Chris stuffed the end of his wrap into his mouth. Kelcy stood up and adjusted the bottom of her shirt. She picked up her coffee cup and shook it.

"I need more coffee." She smiled and made her way to the counter.

A puff of cold air caressed Kelcy's neck, and she stiffened. She remembered what Robert had said. *It can talk to you.* Kelcy placed her mug on the table and shivered, rubbing her arms as she approached the screen door. It had been getting colder day by day, but there had been no need to close the main door yet. The lake looked angry. Its black water reflected the faces of the clouds, the snow disintegrating, eaten by its white teeth. Kelcy moved a chair propping open the solid wooden door. She swung it closed with a soft clank and peered out at the water through its tiny window. Her mind wandered. *You just need to listen.* He repeated.

She stood before the path winding up to his rotting cabin. Snow speckled the ground, melting into the hard soil. The large pine swayed against the sky behind the structure, leaning over his home, then rocking back towards the woods. Robert rocked in his brittle metal chair at the end of his drive. Kelcy turned, her heart fluttering as an empty chair appeared next to his. He waved for her to sit, his phantom limb vibrating, distorting its shape as the snow sank through it, disintegrating into dark mud. Kelcy wasn't sure if the chair was real. Studying its form as she approached. The snow formed small puddles on the seat and she sat on its edge and looked out over the lake.

You have grown. Robert's voice moved between the gusts of icy wind that bellowed through the surrounding woods. Shadows cloaked his pocked, leather-worn face. Moss had grown within its cracks. The fuzzy dark green hairs tickled his features. His orbs seemed to float in their sockets, swaying like rolling waves. Robert smiled, reaching over and patting her hand. Kelcy's heart fluttered and her eyes became wet. Robert smiled and popped a phantom candy in his mouth. The once bright-colored sugar looked decayed and spoiled. He rocked in his chair, observing the snow as it dropped onto the lake's surface.

His mouth pursed as he sucked. *I want to remind you to listen.* He turned towards her. *Listen to the lake. It will tell you everything you need to know.*

Is it dangerous? Her voice trembled, her heart hitching in her chest.

Sometimes. He smiled. *It will return what it has been given, not what it has taken or what has become lost.*

Kelcy gripped his hand and squeezed. She looked at her empty balled fist and then covered her mouth, holding back the fear that gripped her spine. Tears stung her face as the cold air bit into her cheeks.

"You all good?" Chris's voice pulled Kelcy back into the reality of the cabin. She turned away from the door and leaned against the back of a chair. Becky was making another wrap while Seth played with the salt and pepper shakers again.

"Yeah. I'm fine." She pulled the seat and plopped down. Facing away from the door made her anxiety spike, and she folded her hands under the table to keep them from shaking.

Chris nodded and stuffed his mouth. Becky gave him a serious look as he reached for another wrap.

"Well, someone seems to have changed their mind." Becky teased. Chris raised one eyebrow as she twisted her face in a victorious, perverse smile. "People can change, man." He laughed.

PART 2

Chapter 13: Going Underground

The snow continued to fall, creating a blanket of large white orbs that blended into one another as they drifted to the ground. Seth played with the shakers while they cleaned, looking up and smiling when someone would check on him. Chris was assigned to sweeping and leftovers, covering the bowls and plates in cellophane, then stuffing them in the fridge. Becky did the dishes while Kelcy wiped down the counters and table. Seth needed to get ready for bedtime, and Kelcy scooped him up, telling the others she would be right back. Seth waved, then blew Becky and Chris a kiss as he disappeared into the living room. Becky placed her hand on her lips and made a loud smooching sound, throwing the imaginary kiss across the room. Chris gave an awkward smile and continued sweeping the floor. When Kelcy reentered the kitchen, Becky had three fresh cups of coffee waiting. Kelcy questioned if she should drink caffeine this late, assuming that sleep would come like any other night. Random, if at all. So she relented. What would a cup of coffee hurt at this point? Kelcy looked out the window as the snowfall picked up. The small random snowflakes became a thick sheet on her lawn, gathering and mixing with the greens and browns, changing the mood of the landscape. She hadn't seen the lake during the winter months in many years. Kelcy peered out at the treacherous-looking water. The hostile behavior of the waves caused her anxiety to reestablish its grip. Choking her. What was the possibility of being stuck out here? Historically, the snowfall in this part of New York became vicious during this time of year, and Kelcy lacked the ability to prepare. What if they lost power? The cabin had a wood stove in the basement, but her father stopped using it before she was old enough to remember. He had complained, fussing about how much he hated the smell of burning wood. He refused to have his clothes soak up the odor. It reminded him of a campsite. The cabin, now heated and cooled using central air, gave the old structure a modern feel, which her father appreciated. Did he have someone inspect the furnace before she moved back? She would need to call him. Even if the stove was in working order, she didn't see a stockpile of wood anywhere. Where the hell would she get that? She didn't want to ask Chris for another favor, but what other choice was there? She looked over at him, smiling, as he nursed his mug. How would she bring it up? She imagined he would offer to help if she presented her unease. Kelcy knew that Becky and Chris would do anything to ensure the safety of her and her son. Her face flushed when fear made her question herself. Would she have offered help, had the roles been reversed? Probably not. She looked down into her cup, the reflection bending in the brown liquid.

"Do you guys know if the weather is supposed to get worse tonight?" She asked, watching the coffee swirl.

Chris widened his eyes and pulled the corners of his mouth down, staring at the ceiling in contemplation. "I wouldn't think so, but it's upstate New York, so you never know." Becky nodded and sipped from her mug, eyeing Kelcy over the rim.

"If those weather gurus down at channel 78 were ever on point," he continued, "the locals would yell witchcraft."

Kelcy flattened her expression. Becky choked on her coffee and squeezed her mug as she cleared her lungs. Chris raised his glass and smirked, happy that he could offer some comic relief.

"I didn't see a woodpile outside." Chris eyed Kelcy over the rim of his cup. "So you must have a furnace?" Kelcy nodded and looked toward the living room.

"Furnace and wood stove," she confirmed. "But I'm not sure the wood stove is usable."

Chris leaned back in his chair, grinning as if he possessed secret information. He made note of the units spanning the baseboards of the kitchen, and nodded, feeling stupid he hadn't noticed them before.

"You free tomorrow?" He rested the mug of coffee against the top of his sternum. Kelcy nodded, and Chris looked over at Becky. "How about you?" Becky gave him an odd look.

"What do you need me for?" She pulled the corners of her mouth down. What did she know about wood stoves and furnaces? Chris sat up and leaned his elbows on the table.

"I'll need you to take Jr. outside to play while me and Kelcy investigate the furnace and see if this woodstove of hers is in working order." He smiled wider than he needed to. Kelcy nodded, thankful that he had offered before she had to ask.

"I'm pretty sure your father kept up on the furnace maintenance, but we need to check it out." He paused, looking at the table. "May need to call a service guy out here." "Not that I don't know what I'm doing." He averted his eyes, his cheeks flushing. "We will check out this woodstove situation, too." He nodded and sipped from his mug. Kelcy placed her hand on his forearm.

"I appreciate you." She smiled and turned her head toward Becky. "Would that be ok?" Becky became excited.

"Seth is going to love it out there!" She smiled at Kelcy with wide eyes. "Has he ever been out in the snow? Like this kind of snow?" Kelcy shook her head no and Becky clapped her hands together, pointing towards Seth's room. "He is going to love this!" she laughed.

"Make sure you're careful if you go near that lake." Kelcy gripped her cup tight. Becky gave her a sour look and rolled her eyes.

"Are you for real right now?" She teased. "I wouldn't let anything happen to him." She flattened her expression. "I love that boy." She said in a whisper.

"I know," Kelcy smiled. "I just worry."

Becky got up from her seat and raised her arms above her head in a mock cheer as she placed her cup in the sink. She spun around and pointed at Chris. "Okay handyman, eight o'clock sharp." She snapped her fingers. Chris held up his hand in protest.

"Wait, nobody said anything about a time yet." he scrunched his face.

"Eight o'clock," Becky repeated, staring down at him and leaning forward. He held up both hands and laughed.

"Okay." He rolled his eyes and pursed his lips. "Eight o'clock."

Becky clapped her hands again and grabbed her purse from the counter. "I will be here at seven forty-five to help with Seth and breakfast." She trotted toward the door. Kelcy nodded, taking a sip of coffee as she watched Becky out of the corner of her eye. She left without saying another word, and when Kelcy heard the car start, she looked at Chris and puffed her cheeks out.

"I think she likes snow." She laughed, getting up and putting her cup in the sink. She tucked her hands in her pockets and leaned against the counter. Chris took the hint and slapped his palms against his knees. He got up, finished the last mouthful of coffee, and held the cup out before heading for the door.

"Eight o'clock sharp." He said, raising his hand, making a peace sign as she snatched the cup and placed it in the sink. Kelcy stood at the little window as his tail lights faded down the drive. The quietness within the cabin screamed. The ringing in her ears swelled, and she put her hand to her chest to calm the rising anxiety. She needed to lie down. Kelcy headed off toward the other end of the house, pausing as she entered the living room. The basement door ebbed in the darkness, pulsating in her peripheral vision. It made the door seem alive. Like it was breathing. Its wood expanded and contracted within the shadows of the room. The doorknob resembled the eye of a nocturnal beast, glimmering and predatorial. *The cans. Find the cans.* Her voice tickled the back of her skull. Kelcy headed towards Seth's room as the anxiety climbed up her back. She needed to make sure he was asleep before her emotions paralyzed her. Another voice echoed from behind the cabin walls. *Find them Kelcy.* His door creaked as she pressed her arm against the frame, and she froze, peeking through the crack. Seth snored under his blankets, his chest rising and falling in unison with his breathing. She left the door open and went to her bedroom. Kelcy flopped onto her bed and rolled onto her back. The window dragged shadows of twisted arms and falling static, lulling her into a daze. The anxiety swam through her body, pulling her senses into knots. She wrapped her arms around her chest and curled into a ball.

When the pounding woke her up, it took Kelcy a few minutes to focus. She couldn't remember falling asleep, and she wasn't sure what time it was. Muffled yells echoed through the cabin, followed by the pounding. Kelcy fumbled out of bed and shuffled past Seth's room. She peeked in, and the fog cleared, pulling her senses into a state of urgency. He was not in his bed. Rushing into the living room, she slid to a stop, putting her hand over her chest. Seth was sitting on the couch playing with his blocks, slapping them together and making explosion sounds. Kelcy slumped her shoulders as the panic drew in, finding its home in the pit of her stomach. She took a deep breath, trying to calm her nerves as she ambled up next to him.

"Good morning Peapod." she leaned over him, kissing the top of his head.

"Good mormimg Mommy." He smiled, dropping the two blocks into the pile, pulling two more at random. He raised them above his head and then slammed them together, pursing his lips and pushing the air out of his mouth with a popping sound. The pounding on the door made her jerk. Kelcy closed her eyes and tucked a floating strand of hair behind her ear.

"Hang the fuck on!" She yelled, making her way through the kitchen. Pulling open the door, she frowned, looking back and forth in a scowl of hatred. Becky and Chris looked at each other, their smiles fading into disappointment.

"Oof," Chris responded and looked at Becky for affirmation.

"Shut up and make coffee," Kelcy responded as she turned and walked away, plopping herself into a chair and lowering her head to the table, letting her arms dangle.

"Long night?" Becky asked, pulling three coffee mugs from the cupboard. "I can't remember," Kelcy answered, and Becky looked at Chris and shrugged.

"Well," Chris pulled the chair from the table, lowering himself in slow motion as if he were in pain. Kelcy gave him an odd look as Chris settled back, folding his arms behind his head. "Slept wrong." He deflated his chest with a loud exhale and stared at Kelcy. "Why don't you get some coffee and a shower?" When Kelcy didn't respond, Chris continued. "We will get Seth ready and then me and you can check out the basement." Kelcy's breath hitched in her chest. She didn't want to think about it right now. She was hoping Chris would check it on his own. What did he need her for? He didn't. *Find the cans, Kelcy.* She raised her head and sat back in her seat. Random strands of hair covered her half-open eyes. "Yeah, coffee," Chris laughed. *One of them is in the basement, Kelcy.* Her voice tapped at her temple. *Find the cans.*

The voice swirled in her skull, pulsating behind her forehead. *Well, what did your family hide down there? Find the can. You'll see, but you already know, don't you?*

I need you to shut the fuck up. Her voice fought back.

Then shut up. I am just you. She thought to herself.

Becky placed the mug in front of Kelcy and she pulled it to her mouth, taking a huge gulp. She swallowed, raising the mug and nodding.

"Shower," she groaned. "Be right back."

Chris and Becky nodded, giving each other wide-eyed stares. When Kelcy returned, they were at the table with plates of toast, pancakes in the center, and full cups of coffee. Seth sat in his seat, chomping on a triangle of toast. Crumbs littered the front of his dinosaur shirt as he smacked his lips. Clumps of butter gathered at the corners of his mouth.

"Rough night?" Becky asked again, and Kelcy gave her a weary look.

"I laid down and passed out. Don't remember a single thing." She lied, grabbing a pancake and slapping it on her plate, searching the table for syrup. Chris drank his coffee, finishing his piece of toast as he watched Seth eat. He would never want to be a father. He thought children were dangerous. Their fragility and limited fear, oblivious to everything going on around them. The vulnerability of Seth's existence made him uncomfortable. He could never hold that much responsibility for another human being. It was no wonder Kelcy was so stressed all the time.

"I am going to get Seth ready and head out to the yard." Becky got up. She dumped the rest of her coffee in the sink and paused. "He has a jacket, right?" she turned to Kelcy with a look of desperation.

Kelcy stared in amazement. "Yes," she pointed. "Snow pants, boots, and jacket are in the closet." Becky nodded, a look of relief cascading over her face as she crossed the room. "Hat and gloves are in his coat sleeves," Kelcy added and Becky nodded as she opened the closet door. "You know I practically grew up here, right?" Kelcy said with a hint of sarcasm.

Becky pulled the items out and kneeled in front of Seth. "I'm sorry, Kelcy, I wasn't just trying to."

Kelcy interrupted her. "No, I know. Thank you." She smiled. "You are amazing with him. I am tired and being a bitch."

"You said it," Becky smirked, anticipating recourse.

When Kelcy dropped her jaw and scoffed, Becky grinned and bit her bottom lip. "Kidding." She winked. After cleaning Seth's face and hands, she got him dressed and stepped back to look him over. Becky balled her fist and covered her mouth. Kelcy observed the entire ordeal, nodding in approval. Becky thought he looked like the Michelin Man. Chris chuckled and raised his mug, turning his attention to the window above the kitchen sink. The trees swayed as the falling snow circled the air. "Coming down good out there." He grinned.

"Okay." Becky slipped on her jacket and hat, scooped Seth up, and headed towards the porch. "We are off!" she cheered and swung the front door open, looking back and raising her eyebrows. A small gust of snowflakes peppered the floor as the door clanked shut. Kelcy wanted to rush out onto the porch. To make sure they didn't slip on the steps. *What if he fell and hit his head? They were in the middle of nowhere. How would anyone...*

"They will be fine." Chris read her expression.

He put his cup down and stood up, hovering near the table. "Kelcy, you good?" She nodded her head and folded her arms across her chest.

"Yeah," the ends of her mouth turned up in a quiver.

The anxiety itched at her neck, pressing against her throat.

"They will be fine." He smiled.

Kelcy twisted her hands together and took a deep breath. Chris headed into the living room, toward the basement door. Kelcy snapped out of her daze and bolted from the chair, rushing past him. She tucked in close, wrapping her hand around the doorknob. Chris gave her a surprised look. "You first!" He laughed. Kelcy tried to push the anxiety back. *The Butter-Nut cans Kelcy. It's all in the Butter-Nut cans.*

"Shut up." She whispered. Chris leaned in and tilted his head.

"Sorry?" he reached out to put his hand on her shoulder.

Her body was vibrating, and Chris pulled his hand away.

"Nothing." She looked back over her shoulder. Closing her eyes, she turned the knob, clenching her teeth as she swung the door open. The plankboard steps sank into an abyss. A wet, moldy smell seeped from the blackness of its void, and Kelcy stepped back. Without hesitation, Chris stepped past her, trying not to bump into her, and hobbled down the stairs, disappearing into the basement's mouth.

"We may need to purchase a dehumidifier." He called from somewhere in the darkness.

Kelcy held her breath and balled her fists. She wanted answers, and some of them were waiting down there, in the darkness.

Chapter 14: When It Takes

No one had serviced the furnace since its installation in the mid-nineties. Chris picked at the old inspection label and shook his head. He would need a few other tools and some new filters. His expertise lies more in the Angie's List section. A handyman at best. But he could handle this part of the job. They didn't need to call in a specialist, not yet. He assumed once he got digging around, other problems would arise, but he would deal with them as they presented themselves. Dropping his wrench, he clapped his hands together and fanned his flashlight back and forth, inspecting the inside of the furnace. He had given Kelcy his mag light, and she was off somewhere in the far corners of the room, rummaging through shelves and benches. Magazines lay piled three feet high in crates, damp with mildew. Empty oil cans and soda bottles littered the floor. A dirty sheet covered a kitchen table, housing boxes of knickknacks and moldy containers of food. Even if the woodstove worked, he would advise against using it. The room was a fire hazard. He took a break from the furnace, crossing the room to check out the woodstove. The beam of his flashlight flanked in her direction, illuminating Kelcy's back. She hunched over a stack of boxes, extracting items and placing them on the floor next to her feet. Chris tilted the light downward. The beam reflected against a broken music box, with its top missing, resting on its side. Small blackened crates leaned against some rotting magazines. She was looking for something.

"Doing okay over there?" His voice echoed off the walls as he took slow steps toward the woodstove, trying not to trip over the debris. He couldn't remember the last time he had received a tetanus shot, and he wasn't interested in getting one. Kelcy raised a thumbs over her head and then continued digging. Chris turned the light toward the far corner of the room and continued, not surprised by its filthy condition.

Kelcy had fished through several boxes and shelves, finding several Butter-Nut cans, and hesitating before pulling off their lids. Most of them were empty, but a few contained nuts and screws, plastic washers, and even old rusty lures. Kelcy cut her finger a few times, sucking the wounds, hoping to ward off infection. What was she looking for? There was nothing for her to go on except the scattered memories. She concentrated, trying to pull up fragments of her childhood. Did she hold the cans at some point? Did her dad use them to store something, leaving its treasures out for her to see? She froze. *Treasures. Oh, you remember, don't you?* The voice trickled like a leaking faucet, releasing small drips of information. Memories peeled away like an onion. Then the levee broke. The vivid images flooded so quickly that she almost gasped. She turned, twisting the beam around the room. Chris stopped inspecting the stove and flashed his light at her.

"What are you doing?" He covered his face, squinting as her beam flashed by, blinding him.

As Chris watched her scan the room, she twisted her head in frantic movements. He tried to follow her as she weaved back and forth.

"Looking for something to dig with!" She yelled.

Chris pointed his light at the other end of the basement, where he had seen some tools earlier. A peg board, damaged with mold, framed part of the wall. Several tools hung from rusted hooks. Kelcy smiled when she saw the shovel amongst the hedge clippers and claw hammers. She raced across the room, tripping over empty bottles and wet boxes, snatching the shovel off the wall, and heading for the staircase.

"Where are you going?" Chris yelled as she rushed up the stairs.

The light in the kitchen illuminated the basement floor and Chris shook his head as he turned back to the wood stove. "Always something." He mumbled and knocked his knuckles on the thick steel frame. The sound echoed through the basement, and he reached for the door handle and gave it a hard twist.

Kelcy left the house and almost toppled down the stairs as she scanned the yard. She didn't see Seth or Becky as she made her way toward the back of the cabin. She scanned left and right down the length of the road and then looked toward the shoreline. Fear rose into her chest, making her heave. The snow blinded her vision of the lake, but she heard the water biting the shore. She was unsure where they might have gotten off to, and she closed her eyes, trying to hinder the intrusive thoughts. Kelcy circled the backside of the cabin and paced the boundary of the woods. A memory pulled forward. A tree. She could picture the infant pine in her head. That was why he had picked that sapling, to hide things. By now, the tree would be enormous.

Sly girl, you remember.

She was playing in the backyard when they delivered the baby pine. The sapling was already several feet taller than her, and she stared wide-eyed as they placed the bundled roots in the hole.

Oh, it grew so grand. Yes. Easy to hide things.

She clenched her eyes shut for a moment, cursing her voice to shut up. Kelcy passed each tree, walking back and forth, studying their base. She was looking for a rock. Memories flashed in quick phantom movies. He had buried the can near a rock. Under a rock or near a rock? She shook her head and tried to force the information forward. During her second pass around the perimeter, she spotted it. She covered her mouth as the images flooded forward. *Near a rock.* Snow covered the stone. A patch of moss poked out from under a white blanket as the breath plumed from her lungs. She raised the shovel and squeezed the handle tighter, slamming down hard. Kelcy's heart fluttered when the blade dug into the earth. The moving images in her mind played on. She had come upon her grandfather digging a hole and he had said it was his Daddy's treasure.

"These items are important things that need to be stored away. Somewhere safe." He smiled, pressing his finger to his lips, promising her an entire bag of saltwater taffy if she kept it a secret. She was only digging for a few minutes when the tip of the shovel clanked against something hard. Kelcy fell to her knees and scooped the dirt aside. Faded red paint bled against the snow. A sickness formed in the pit of her stomach as she pried the can from the earth and wiped the dirt from its sides. Her hands trembled as she smeared her thumb across the white bold label. Butter-Nut Coffee. She tilted the can, digging her nails into the edges of its metal lid. It held in place, and she cussed as she reached for the shovel. Kelcy placed the handle under her knee and shifted her weight. Tilting the crease of the can's lid on the tip of the shovel, she took a deep breath and held it. With a solid *wack*, the lid popped off and partially disappeared under the snow. She peered inside, then dropped the can, scooting backward. Bile worked its way up her throat as tears blurred her vision. She buried her head in her chest and hugged her knees.

Look what you found!

Is that...

Yes, it is...go get it and have another look.

Kelcy raised her head, wiping her wrist across her eyes. Fear choked the sobs as she crawled back to the can and tipped it upright. She looked in and covered her mouth again. Anxiety climaxed. Her chin quivered as her throat clenched shut, stifling her scream.

"Mommy?" A voice shot across the yard from behind her. Kelcy spun around to see Seth standing by the side of the cabin, alone. Kelcy ran the back of her hand over her eyes and sat up on her knees.

"Where is Becky?" Her voice trembled, scanning the yard behind him. She grabbed the can and shuffled around in the snow until she found the lid, never taking her eyes off Seth. "Stay there, Peapod, okay?" She pressed the lid in place, smacking it with her palm, and scrambled on her hands and knees to her son. He twisted his head upright and stuck out his tongue, collecting the snowflakes that danced around his head. "Where is Becky, Peapod?" She looked him over. Making sure he wasn't hurt. Seth turned and pointed toward the water.

"She's in the lake, Mommy." He smiled. Kelcy stared at him. She wasn't sure that she heard him correctly and looked into his eyes for confirmation. Chris stepped out into the yard, holding a red canister in his hands. His eyes were wide with panic. Seth looked back and smiled. Chris looked away, hugging the can to his chest.

Oh, he found the other can! Her voice teased.

Kelcy stood up, pressing Seth against her leg.

"Where's Becky?" Chris stared. His eyes resembled polished marbles. The snow reflected from their glossy surface as the snowflakes melted into his flushed visage. Seth pointed toward the lake, and Chris craned his neck, looking back down the hill. The waves snapped the ice sheet that had formed at the shore of the beach. He looked down at the canister. The shock had manifested into fear and choked his ability to react.

"Kelcy," his voice sounded distant as it echoed across the backyard. Kelcy gripped her son's hand, and he pulled her forward, maneuvering past Chris. She followed him up the porch and into the house, placing the can on the kitchen table. Kelcy removed his winter clothes as he smiled and clapped his hands.

"Cartoons Mommy." He pointed and ran toward the television.

She tried to control her emotions, swallowing the lump in her throat, as she hung up his clothes and followed him to the living room. Seth climbed onto the sofa, cuddling under an oversized couch pillow as Kelcy grabbed the remote.

"Why is she in the lake, Peapod?" Her voice sounded distant. Foreign.

Seth stared at the screen as the animations danced in his eyes.

"Peapod?" she repeated.

Her voice trembled. Kelcy swallowed, knotting her hands together. He shrugged his shoulders and giggled as the tom cat chased the little mouse under a table, smacking the top of his head against the wood, and collapsing to his belly. Kelcy stared at Seth as her entire body vibrated.

"Don't come outside, okay?" She bent down and kissed his forehead.

Grabbing the can from the kitchen table, she rushed back outside. Kelcy found Chris down by the shore when she came out onto the porch. Her anxiety dug its heels in, climbing her spine and resting on the back of her neck.

He found the can in the basement. The one with his things.

Kelcy pinched her eyes closed as the world tilted. She wanted to vomit. Her stomach clenched as her voice hissed from the base of her neck.

I would have wanted you to find it first, but you remembered. Oh, you remembered Grandaddy didn't you? It is amazing what the sons of the father will do, isn't it?

Gripping her stomach, she waddled down the drive, watching as Chris's form ebbed in her vision. The carnival sounds from the cabin spilled from the doorway and echoed out over the lake.

Daddy knows too. A quiet laugh emanated from the depth of her mind. *It's why he had to get rid of that pesky yard worker. You will find them in there. All the secrets.*

Kelcy leaned forward, splashing the snow with her stomach contents.

Just mow the lawn, you little shit, but nooooo, you had to dig more than the flowerbeds, didn't you? So he sends his brother while he gets his nose dirty.

"Shut the fuck up." She dropped the can and pressed her palms against her temples. Squeezing so hard, she thought her head might pop. She leaned over and scooped up the can, hugging it to her chest as she took staggered steps down the drive. Chris stood at the shore, staring into the lake as if in a trance. Kelcy spit and wiped her mouth with the sleeve of her shirt as she made her way to the beach.

"Chris?" His name bounced on her swollen tongue. Forcing it to come out sloppy. She approached him from behind, pausing within an arm's length. Her head felt like a lead weight. An overwhelming notion of dread gripped her, causing her knees to wobble. Chris stared into the foaming water, his eyes wide in terror. The small waves licked the ice sheet. There was no sign of Becky. No lifeless face, staring back in horror, mouth agape in a scream. No hair swirling around her submerged head. Arms splayed outward as if she were playing dead man's float. She was just gone.

"Chris?" She circled to his side as he continued to search the waves. The red canister pressed into the sand at his feet, mirrored hers. His eyes, swollen with tears, vibrated as they rotated in their sockets. The pupils dilated as they focused on Kelcy.

His lips quivered as his chin pulled down. A thin line of spittle stretched, bending in the icy breeze.

"He killed my brother." He hissed. Clenching his fists.

The swaying string of mucus broke and slapped against his shirt as Kelcy sank to her knees in the wet sand. Looking down at the black, soot-covered lid, she hugged the can to her chest.

Chapter 15: Dredging

The tin cans looked flat in the low light of the kitchen. Kelcy placed them in the center of the table and stared at the bright red label with bulky white lettering. Seth giggled from the living room as animated sounds leaked in, filling the void. Kelcy formed the words in her throat several times. Pushing the sound past the anxiety that suppressed any sense of reality.

"My father? He killed Mark?" Her mouth was like sandpaper, and she licked her lips.

His eyes looked like black orbs as he focused on the can he found in the basement. He slumped forward, his back arching, pulling his spine tight against his shirt. Kelcy thought he resembled something wicked. His face became twisted. Something evil. Chris mumbled words Kelcy couldn't hear, and she leaned in toward him.

"Your family." He said under his breath. As he clenched his mouth shut, his lips drew a thin line across his face. "There is something wrong with your family." He continued. The accusation slashed at her heart. He directed the words at her as if she held some of the blame. She had nothing to do with her family's past. She closed her eyes, allowing the words to cascade over her shoulder. Rage consumed him. She needed to let him talk. Chris placed his right hand on the table and turned, focusing on the can again. Kelcy opened her eyes, not daring to look at him.

"I'm sorry." He bowed his head. "I just."

Kelcy took a deep breath and placed her hand on his forearm. The vibration from his body surged into her as his shoulders relaxed. They would need to deal with the contents of the cans, but all she could do was stare at them.

"What should we do about this?" she bit her bottom lip, wanting to scream. Chris huffed, his chest rising and collapsing into his weight.

"I don't know," he whispered.

Kelcy bit down harder, drawing blood as the words spilled out.

"There's a finger of a child in there." Her eyes remained glued to the bright red label.

Chris sat up straight. He focused on her coffee tin. His breathing became labored. "There is a barrette in there, definitely a child's, and some newspaper clipping of a young girl." She continued.

Air pressed from Chris's lungs. His throat hitched as he tried to say something, tears cascading down his pale face. He turned away, and Kelcy squeezed his forearm tight. The room swayed as her anxiety pulled at reality.

When he spoke, his voice was almost a whisper.

"There is a letter," he reached across the table, pulling a napkin from the dispenser. "I only read some of it." He sobbed, averting his face as he wiped his eyes and blew his nose. His voice echoed off the walls, and Kelcy looked towards the living room. The colorful lights from the television washed the wooden floors and Seth's giggles overlapped the exaggerated sound effects of playful violence. "And a polaroid." His chest heaved again. Kelcy let go of his forearm and reached for his can. Its light weight surprised her. As if it contained only air. Chris put his head in his arms and wept as she pulled off its lid. She tilted the can and peered over the rim. Kelcy reached in and pulled out a folded piece of paper, water-stained and ragged. She placed it on the table and looked back toward the living room again, making sure Seth's attention remained occupied. Kelcy tried to steady her nerves. A photograph slid out. The weathered and cracked Polaroid revealed two bare legs tied together with twine. She gagged, covering her mouth. Kelcy's tongue stuck to the roof of her mouth as she scanned the photo. The victim's arms appeared tied behind his back. Purple and blue bruises climbed his right limb from the wrist to the elbow. Large circular spots of blood stained his ripped Rolling Stone t-shirt. The logo's huge red lips and tongue blended with the visceral tone of gore. She dropped the photo and swallowed the bile climbing her esophagus. The mucus had a hint of acid that burned her throat. She gagged again, closing her eyes tight, trying to keep her stomach contents from rising. Kelcy recognized Mark's face. His eyes stared back at her, wide in shock. The visage had large cuts across its mouth, creating a mock smile. His tongue lay half carved out of a gaping maw of missing teeth. Vomit rushed up, and she turned, moving to the sink, expelling herself into the metal basin. She leaned over, gasping.

Your father is a bad, wicked man. The voice laughed.

Kelcy squeezed her eyes closed as her face trembled. She heard the popping sound of a lid and then Chris moaning.

Bradley, I need you. Kelcy focused on the bottom of the basin.

Bright pink contents painted against polished steel snaked down the drain as the sweet smell of stomach acid filled her nostrils. There were footsteps, and the door swinging open. A chill swept the backside of her legs. A clank killed the breeze, and Kelcy leaned her full weight against the counter and turned on the faucet.

Please, Bradley. I need you. She continued to summon him.

Kelcy listened to the hum of running water and cupped her hands, shoveling it into her mouth, and swirling it before spitting it out. The snow was heavy, falling fat puffs as she walked out onto the porch. She approached the stairs and looked out over the yard, not daring to look toward the lake. Afraid that Becky would lunge from its depths, arms outstretched, reaching for her. Chris stood with his hands in his pockets, eyes focused on the shoreline.

"Where is she?" His voice was sharp and angry.

Confused by the question, Kelcy tilted her head.

"Seth said she went into the lake." Her voice sounded strange now. Her head buzzed with tension as a sense of madness overtook her, pulling her from her body.

Chris bit his bottom lip. "She wouldn't walk out into the lake and drown herself."

Kelcy looked over her shoulder towards the living room. Her gut twisted into a knot. He cleared his throat, squaring his shoulders.

"We need to call the police." He faced her. Kelcy nodded as Chris pulled his cell phone from his pocket. She reached out, draping her fingers over his forearm.

"Only about Becky." Her eyes were pleading, a sudden fear cascading over her face. Chris bowed his head and rubbed his thumb over the phone's metallic covering.

"You can't hide what he has done, Kelcy." He lowered his voice and stared at his hands. Her throat tightened. He was right. They wouldn't be able to hide this, even if she wanted to.

"I need to confront him first. Please." She squeezed and looked into his eyes. "I need him to confess, Chris. Please."

He looked out over the lake and then pressed on the phone's keypad. He brought the phone to his ear and Kelcy held her breath as panic festered to an almost uncontrollable level. Her arms shook when she heard the stale voice of the dispatch.

"911, what's your emergency?"

Chris paused, his mouth half open. He stared into Kelcy's eyes. He tilted his head and looked out over the lake.

"I need to report a missing person." He pinched the brim of his nose. Chris knew this decision was going to bite him in the ass, but it was for her. He took a few steps away, and Kelcy strained to make out the conversation, his voice fading into mumbles. "It seems she may have fallen into the lake," he nodded. Kelcy listened as he shook his head and gave as many details as he could, leaving out what he had promised. When he flipped the phone shut, Kelcy approached, and Chris held his hand up. She backed away as he headed back into the cabin, slamming the door behind him.

Reds and blues bounced off the cabin walls, strobing against the kitchen ceiling. Kelcy held Seth on her lap as they sat around the table. The officer leaned in, tapping his pen against his notepad and staring at them with a flat expression. Chris had known Billy Jessle since he was five years old. They had met on the playground of Argyle Central School, becoming fast friends while bullying other kids. Taking their lunches, stealing pencils during class, and starting fights in the hallways. Throughout their childhood, if things happened in this town, they were the first two kids the cops came looking for. When they graduated high school, Billy told Chris he was thinking about going to school for criminal justice. Chris laughed at the irony, reassuring Billy that if he went through with it, he better put him on the "do not fuck with" list.

Over the years, they bumped into each other but never rekindled their friendship. Things change, people change, and neither of them resembles who they once were. Chris hadn't recognized him when he stepped onto the porch. He gained a solid twenty pounds of muscle and sported a huge graying bushy beard. Chris thought he looked like a Santa Claus on steroids. Billy's thin sandy blonde hair receded halfway to the back of his skull and Chris smiled, trying not to stare at it.

"So this is the summer camp girl you were all gaga about when we were kids?" Billy teased, trying to lighten the mood of the room. When Chris gave him an irritated look, Billy cleared his throat and squeezed his beard. His smile pulled into a thin line that disappeared beneath his mustache.

"So explain this to me again, Chris?" Billy focused his attention and continued to tap his pencil against the pad. He dropped his gaze to her son and gave him a wide smile. Seth bounced up and down on Kelcy's lap and then waved. Billy winked and waved back. Chris itched the tabletop with his index finger and shot Kelcy a glance.

"When I came into the yard, Kelcy was kneeling next to Seth and he was pointing toward the lake," Chris repeated the details more clearly this time.

Billy scribbled on his notepad and nodded.

"I was in the basement when I heard," he continued.

"Right," Billy cut him off. "You were in the basement doing what?"

Chris looked over at Kelcy. "I was checking out her woodstove. To make sure it was safe to use for the winter." Kelcy nodded, confirming the information. Billy eyed the electric units that ran across the kitchen floorboards and gave Chris a strange look. He looked back at the units and clicked his tongue between his teeth.

"And is it safe?" he asked.

"No." Chris smiled. He looked at Kelcy and folded his hands. He adjusted his position and continued. "Then I heard them out in the yard." He finished.

Billy looked at Kelcy and stared hard. "And this is all accurate so far?"

Kelcy nodded and bounced Seth on her lap. The anxiety dug into her neck as her heartbeat throbbed in her ears.

"What was the sound exactly?" Billy flipped the page on his pad, and looked up at Chris, waiting for his reaction.

"I yelped, I guess," Kelcy answered for Chris, keeping her eyes fixated on her son.

"You guess?" The officer scribbled and tapped the eraser against the pad. Each slap stabbed her brain, making her wince.

"And the boy was with Miss Brendle, your nanny." He looked over the notes on the previous page. "Down by the lake?" He reiterated.

Kelcy nodded, and Billy smiled, scribbling more notes. He set the pad down and folded his fingers together on the table.

"Why on earth would she be down there by the lake with your son?" He leaned in.

The shock from his question made Kelcy open and close her mouth like a fish. She needed to stay calm.

It was a stroll down by the lake. Just say that. Her inner voice teased. *Tell him your son loved the snow, and she took him down by the lake so he could watch her die!* Panic pressed on her chest, and Chris looked over at her and grinned.

"She took him for a walk, as they do most days," Chris interjected, returning the favor. Kelcy smiled at him and Chris turned his focus back to Billy.

"Is this information correct, Miss Caldwell?" Billy closed one eye. Kelcy lifted Seth, hugging him to her chest as she stood up.

"Yes," she smiled. "Becky took him out for walks every day." Seth hugged her neck. "If you will excuse me, I need to put my son to bed. It's getting late." Billy looked at his notepad and smiled.

"Do you mind if I talk to Chris out on the porch a moment before I leave, Miss Caldwell?"

Kelcy nodded and bounced Seth against her hip, giving Chris a stern glare.

"I'll be back in a moment," Chris said as Kelcy walked into the living room. Billy nodded and pushed his seat back. They stepped out onto the porch, and Billy waited for Chris to shut the door before he continued.

"I'll be back out in a few days." He adjusted his belt. "There may be a search team out here tomorrow, but I can't guarantee it. Small town, small funding, you know." He slapped Chris on the shoulder. "I suspect you are familiar with what comes next, Chris." He straightened his posture and looked back toward the door. "Please tell Miss Caldwell not to leave town."

Chris nodded and scuffed his foot against the floorboards. The sun fell behind the trees, painting the sky orange. Distant white caps fought against the forming ice sheet, causing the lake to war with itself. The snowfall was becoming thicker, and they stood in silence as their breath created clouds.

"Are you putting me in an awkward position?" Billy put his hands in his pockets and teetered on the edge of the top step.

Chris looked out over the lake, not sure if the chill that ran up his spine was from the cold or his guilt. He looked over at Billy and nodded.

"I wasn't out here when she disappeared, Billy."

Billy nodded and kicked his boot against the snow-covered wood. He wanted to make sure Chris understood he had a job to do. Nothing personal. If information was being suppressed, he would figure it out. He also knew strange things happened out here.

"I know it's been a long time since we ran the streets together, Chris, but I would like to think we have a pretty solid understanding of each other." Chris kept his eyes on the frigid waters.

"I can't help you if there's more to this than what you're telling me. We understand each other?" Billy ascended in slow steps, leaving Chris to his thoughts as he made his way to the police cruiser. He opened the driver's side door and looked up. "I'll be back out." He smiled. "Call me if something's on your mind." Chris nodded as he climbed into his cruiser. The engine split the silence of the lake, and Chris listened to his heart thud against his chest plate as Billy pulled down the drive and turned onto the main road.

Chapter 16: What he has done

Kelcy lay in bed, watching the shadows from the falling snow dance across the ceiling. Chris had warned her that Billy expected things were not on the up and up and she would need to come clean. Her heart ached as it beat against her chest plate. Kelcy closed her eyes and tried to relax, but the darkness would pulsate behind her eyelids, causing her anxiety to swell. Becky's bloated and twisted form appeared in the shadows of the room. Her opaque eyes, cloudy and lifeless, focused and pleading for help. Her limbs defied gravity, contorting from the dark corners of the room. There was the terrible notion that itched at Kelcy's conscience. What if Becky's body remained undiscovered? Her story would disappear within the fabric of the lake's folklore, like the rest of this godforsaken place, and Kelcy would be able to slip away with her child, disappearing into obscurity. Her narcissism mortified her and if this all ended badly; she deserved it. Whether they find Becky. If she exposed her father, the people here would forever remember them as evil, affirming what they already believed. That they were a blight, a sickness. What would happen to Chris? Would she ever see him again? She couldn't blame him for the hate he harbored towards her family. He would have been better off running her over that day. But she would have saved Seth from all of this. They would move far away. Living a secluded life somewhere in Vermont or Maine.

Oh, you can't escape. It is a part of you now. Robert's voice cut through the darkness, seeping from within the walls of the cabin. A sense of dread gripped Kelcy, and she sucked her lips inward as tears pooled, clouding her vision. Her brow ached as she clamped her eyes shut.

"What am I supposed to do?" She whispered in the darkness.

Listen to the lake. Listen to her.

"Why?" she asked.

Because it knows things. Within its beauty, there is darkness. It will give back what it is given. Robert whispered, the warning cascading across the ceiling.

Kelcy crossed her arms and rocked back and forth, sobbing, as she hugged her chest under the cold sheet. What was happening? She felt as if she might lose her mind. Ghosts telling her to listen to a cursed lake while her friends died around her. Her great grandfather, a killer? Her grandfather handed it down to her dad like a sick family heirloom, and he continued the ritual with Mark. The reality of her situation was more horrific than the folklore. Her sanity unraveled, as she became sick. Would she become like them? The curse demanding to be continued? When they come for her, they will take Seth away and lock her up. That's what happens with crazy people. They get put away. Far away.

Be brave. Robert's voice slithered behind shadows. *Listen to the lake.*

"What is it supposed to tell me, Robert?" She pleaded. Her voice was faint as if the words were floating somewhere far away from where she lay. The sweet smell of candy engulfed the room, and behind her eyelids, a bright light pulsed in rhythm with her heartbeat. She clenched her eyes tighter, fear threatening to snap her brain in two.

The lake gives back what it has been given. Listen to it. Watch its teeth. His words caressed her face before fading into the ether.

The light from the window flickered, causing the room to strobe behind her eyelids. When Kelcy opened her eyes, the ceiling reflected the speckled shadows of the falling snow. She sat up in her bed gasping, covered in sweat. Pulling back the sheets, she swung her legs over the side of the bed and placed her feet against the cold wooden floors. She rubbed her hands along the edge of the bed, assuring her balance before she tried to stand up. Her anxiety pulled her back towards the mattress, but she couldn't let it take her. She needed to read that letter.

At two in the morning, Kelcy pulled the folded water-stained paper from its canister. Her hands trembled as she unfolded the first crease. She flattened the corners, pressing her fingers hard against them, trying to keep the edges from bending back up. Her mouth held a metallic taste, and the low lighting of the kitchen teased her anxiety. Something evil crept from the paper when it crackled, like breaking a seal on an old parchment of spells. But she didn't believe in witchcraft. This harbored something darker. As she unfolded the last section, Kelcy ran her fingers over the crude handwriting and closed her eyes. When she was ready, she looked down at the page and read his confession.

If you have spent time within its waters, you understand the lake's pull. The attraction of its beauty. I came here to cleanse myself of my ailments, and for some time it had worked. The lake kept me busy. Slipping my urges into a daydream. Tourists came in droves during the summer months, and I had no time to indulge in my darker thoughts. Now that I am alone, away from the lake, I have nothing but them to punish me.

I tried to fill the slower winter months with ski trips around the lake's shorelines. Sometimes, if the weather was calm, I would take the vacationers across the middle. I felt like I was offering them something more. A taste of what we are blessed with every day. I was always careful, and we were always safe. Its teeth. Frozen under lock and key. Unable to bite. The visitors would stare down into the abyss as if they had never seen something so mesmerizing. City folk. When you focus on the deep blue of its soul, it shows you just how small you are in the grand scheme of things; I think. This is my life. The lake. My work. I hoped it would keep me at arm's length from myself and I embraced this place with my entire soul. Until she came.

If you were to have asked me, during those years, if there would have been anything that would have separated me from the serenity of the lake. From my cure. I would call you a fool and send you on your way. But I was wrong. The lake could have never saved me from myself. It could only blind me from my true nature. Like a well-trained pony, guided toward the correct path, only whipped when necessary. It kept me in line for as long as it could. As long as I could. It happened when I had become bored with whitling that day. Well, as they say, idle hands. I spent hours carving figurines of little fish and turtles, which I gave away to children during fishing trips and winter festivities. It allowed me some satisfaction. Kept me honest. Allowed me to believe that I had cast out my demons. Or at least locked them away. That I could safely be around them. As I said, I had grown bored that day. Too bored, and the breeze off the lake called to me, so, I took a walk along the North road.

Her name was Sophia. I honestly never knew her age, but the papers had reported her as nine years old when she went missing. She was the child of one of those Russian tourists we would get every year during the summer. Her big blue eyes made her face look like a small angel and her vibrant blonde hair, held tight against her head with bright barrettes, seemed iridescent in the sunlight. I still have one of her hair clips hidden away in my bedroom closet in an old coffee can.

Kelcy paused, looking up at the Butter-Nut label. A sickness swelled in her stomach and she swallowed the thick mucus that formed on the pallet of her tongue as she continued to read.

I want to write this down so my family knows what the lake can do. It was watching me that day. Our exchange. The way I smiled and waved, that Devil moving my tongue to form the salutations. The waves slapped the shoreline, hissing as I grabbed her and dragged her into the woods. I do not know what came over me. I had kept control for so long. The vile urge that festered behind my mind's eye just took over, I guess. I thought I had caged its power, but I had no proper control, it seems. That Devil had seized my limbs, covering her mouth with my rough hands, throwing her to the ground, and wrapping them like hooks around her small, frail neck.

I must have sat there for hours with her lifeless body twisted amongst the leaves. A few vacationers had walked past, and I watched them stroll by, laughing and conversing about God knows what, oblivious to the hell that lay only a few yards away. I waited until it became dark, and the moonlight danced in her bulging eyes. Its beauty memorized me, and I said as much. Maybe it was an illusion, but I had never seen it so tranquil. The nocturnal eye of God ebbing from within the lifeless orbs of one of his children.

I had stood in the woods, afraid, alone with her in the darkness. I knew someone would find her eventually. Her remains. Dragged into the road by dogs or other woodland creatures. Her half-eaten vessel. A reminder of the lake's potential horrors. Maybe that would be the tragedy those news people would report. The familiar tale of the unattended child wandering into the woods. Lost. But someone could discover the truth. The wounds around her neck were now visible in the moonlight. The signs of things worse than happenstance. Monsters, unlike the ones that nibble the flesh from bone, lurk amongst the inhabitants of the lake. Me.

I was careful when I picked her up. She was so fragile, her limbs twisted and bent in unnatural ways. I had to put her down and expel my stomach contents in the bushes. When I had regained my composure, I carefully coddled her in my arms and made my way to the shore. She looked as if she were sleeping, protected within a dream. Safe from the nocturnal beasts that roamed the woods. Placing her on the sand, I let the lake taste her flesh, its white teeth frothed around her shoulders. Carefully, I removed the barrette and slipped it into my pocket, feeling a sense of elation. I can't recall why I needed it so desperately. I just need things, I guess. As a reminder, perhaps. Her golden locks drifted into the churning tide, spreading like a crown above her head.

Something had come over me then. I have no explanation for it, any more than a prodding urge. Another need. Without premeditation, I searched the sand for a tool. Something sharp. I became frantic, picking up sticks and flinging them disappointed into the mouth of the lake. For a moment, I felt like my world was spiraling out of control. Then I felt the pocket knife press against my leg. I remember pulling the tool and opening the blade to the moon. I needed more. Something more than bright plastic. That Devil, I have no other name which to call it, lunged me forward, grasping her small hand. It pulled her index finger out and, with one swipe, nipped it from her body. The bright foam darkened with her ichor as the Devil inside me laughed. It shoved the appendage into my pocket as a rush of energy surged through my body. It was a sense of euphoria I could never explain, even now, in my old age.

Plucking stones from the lake, we stuffed them into her clothes. I walked her out as far as I could, then pushed her under the water, and let the lake take her, not knowing then what it could do. I returned to my cabin, the Devil quelled, and wrapped the finger in a cloth, placing it into the can with the barrette. Tucking it in the freezer, I had gone to bed. I needed rest. I needed to come down from it all. It had been so long since I had let the feelings take control. Let the Devil have its way.

Her parents had reported her missing the following day, and I, like others, joined in the search. I traipsed through the woods, knowing full well where she lay, blessing the lake for its kindness in keeping our secret. Our exchange. By the end of that summer, the authorities had abandoned hope. The family had stayed for a few more months, searching the woods alone. I am not sure when they left.

When I had taken the group to the fishing holes that winter, the storm had been building since morning. It came in small gusts, but I felt it would be safe enough to take them through the middle. Let them gawk over the cavities. The men had gone to shore, and I watched as the drifts of snow plumed, swirling into small tornados across the ice. When the first scream echoed from the void, my spine tightened. I watched as she reached from beneath the ice, tearing the bodies apart. Vibrant sprays of red luster painted across a white background. I saw a man pull a knife. His arm was twisted and torn from its socket, in a spray of essence. It was her. I saw her peer up at me from under the glass lid of her tomb. Her black orbs reflected milky and white from beneath. Tendrils drifted. Spreading out like snakes from the space where a barrette once clasped her hair. I watched in horror as she took them all. I waited for her to come for me, but she faded beneath the ice, leaving me amongst the gore. Approaching a fishing hole, I sat and slid my feet into the waters, pleading for her to take me too, but she would not. She had now taken her trophy to remind herself of what I had done that night at the lake. What I had abandoned to it. I have cursed this place and probably my entire bloodline, but I cannot stop what I am. I cannot fix what I have done.

The kitchen light flickered, the shadows of the cabin forming into fictitious creatures. Kelcy needed to call her father. She needed to find Chris. She needed to get her son the hell away from this lake.

Chapter 17: Mourning Time

Several emergency vehicles and police cruisers huddled the shoreline when Chris arrived at the cabin the next morning. Memories flooded forward. Recalling details of his brother's search and rescue as he pulled up the driveway. He studied them from his side mirror, imagining them pulling Becky's remains from the gray mouth of the lake. He closed his eyes and tried to shake the thought. Kelcy looked down at him from her perch and sipped at her coffee. Chris sat in his truck for a few minutes, eyeing the search team. He twisted the key, killing the engine, and stared up at her. Kelcy nodded as he climbed out of the truck, pinching the brim of his hat as he approached. The sound of cartoons echoed from deep within the cabin, and Chris leaned to the side, stretching his back.

"He doing ok?" he asked, careful how his words came out.

The mix of joy emanating from the cabin and the chaos of reality down at the beach harbored an overwhelming tension.

"He is doing fine." Kelcy smiled and stood up, heading back into the kitchen. Chris looked over his shoulders.

An officer climbed empty handed from the icy waters, shaking his head. Chris headed up the steps. Kelcy reappeared, extending a fresh cup of coffee before returning to her perch on the top step. He sat next to her and squeezed the mug in his palms.

"We have to tell them about your father, Kelcy." He kept his eyes focused on the man in the wet suit, nodding and adjusting his gear as officers stood around him. A few other divers waded waist-high in the frozen water, waiting for orders. Kelcy held up her hand in protest and gave him an evil eye.

"I need to speak to him first. I need you to understand that, Christopher." She looked over, glaring at him.

The way she said his first name in full, dragging out the last few syllables, made Chris clench his jaw. She sounded like his mother. He understood her position, but her father was a murderer. Did she assume he would confess over the phone? A full confession by Daddy dearest? He gripped his mug, feeling the need to throw it across the yard. What then? Daddy would hand himself over to the authorities? No harm, no foul. The whole thing was absurd. He wanted to march down to the beach and point up at the cabin. Tell the officers they were looking for answers in the wrong place. He didn't believe Kelcy held back the information out of malice or some weird savior complex. Like him, she wanted answers. Chris took a sip of his coffee and let the acidity burn into his tongue before he swallowed. He cleared his throat and focused on the brown swirling liquid in his mug.

"Are you going to just ask him?" He blurted out.

Kelcy bowed her head and sighed. She wasn't sure what she was going to do, but it would not be without proper planning. Her father killed Mark, her great-grandfather killed a little girl, and her grandfather kept the secret like some twisted family heritage. Did the wives know about what their men had done? Did they help? Her hand trembled, and she tightened the grip around her mug.

"I am going to confront him, but I don't know how yet, Chris." She looked up at the shoreline. A few of the officers were talking to a diver standing ankle deep in the water. "If he denies it." She paused and looked at her feet. Kelcy turned to him and gave Chris a stern look. "You can call it in."

There would be no compromise. He needed to let her find her way through it. What he needed to focus on was being an ally, not an enemy. The truth of what happened to Mark remained unknown, and now that he knew, there was no rush for justice. It would come. If not by her hands, then his. Chris nodded, caressing his mug as the divers pulled their face masks down and waded back into the water, disappearing under the ice sheet.

Kelcy checked in on Seth, bringing him a sandwich and a glass of milk as he bounced on the sofa. He kicked his feet out and landed on his backside, giggling as he slid up to the coffee table and snatched a square of bread. He studied the edges before taking a huge bite.

"Fank you Mommy." He smiled up with jelly and peanut butter collected on the corners of his mouth.

"You're welcome, Peapod." She smoothed his hair and looked toward the television. "Mommy has to make a phone call, k, you watch cartoons, and Mommy will be right back." Seth nodded and took a larger bite. Chris remained on the porch, staring at the crew on the beach. She instructed him to come get her if anything changed. She was unwilling to say Becky's name. The thought caused a lump to form in her throat. He nodded, understanding full well what she had meant. He couldn't say her name out loud, either.

The rotary phone on the nightstand next to the bed looked morbid. She imagined his voice, amplifying from it like a bullhorn.

"Good to hear from you kiddo, how is it going up there?"

She would be straightforward. "Why did you kill Mark?" she would ask.

The pause in his voice, as the air between them thickened to an insurmountable horror, and the click as the buzz rang into her skull. The siren of guilt.

Kelcy pushed the little nub into the door and shook the handle to ensure it was locked. When she approached the side of the bed, her knees buckled, forcing her to sit. The ends of her fingers tingled as she pulled the receiver, placing the hard plastic against her ear. Her finger trembled as she inserted the appendage into the slot. Kelcy twisted each number; the ticking screaming into the void of the room. She hovered over the last digit. Her tongue pressed flat against the roof of her mouth. She closed her eyes and dialed. There was a click, followed by a rattle and dial tone. The beeps, each brighter and louder than its predecessor, made her squeeze her eyes closed until her face scrunched up into a tight ball. A final click resonated, and his voice broke the line.

"Hello?" His familiar timbre flooded her ear.

Kelcy's breath hitched, and she placed her hand on her chest.

"Dad?" Her voice trembled.

"What's the matter, kiddo? Everything ok up there? You sound upset." He chirped in a happy cadence.

Her mouth quivered as the tears welled. Her tongue felt heavy against her breath.

"Kelcy?" his voice became serious. "What is going on? Is Seth okay?"

Kelcy opened her eyes and stared into the depths of the blurry room.

"Why did you kill Mark?" She pursed her lips.

The silence hissed from the earpiece of her receiver.

"What are you talking about?" His tone had taken on a sudden agitation.

The trembling of her neck made the words come out, fumbled. "I found the cans, dad." She raised her hand to her mouth as she emptied her lungs. "I found the fucking cans." She raised her voice, speaking in a sharp tone.

There was another stretch of silence, and Kelcy clenched her fists, waiting for him to explode. She opened her mouth, and he interrupted her.

"I will be there as soon as I can." He hissed. "Don't you fucking move."

The line went dead.

When Kelcy walked out, officer Jessle was standing at the crest of the steps in front of Chris. He mumbled something before turning his attention to her, pulling a professional smile. Chris eyed Billy and then turned toward Kelcy with a grave expression.

"I'm sorry Miss Caldwell." He turned his gaze to his feet. "We have found no trace of Miss Brendle yet, and we assume the currents may have dragged her to the center of the lake." He cleared his throat. "Tides and all." He added.

Kelcy nodded and put her hands in her pockets. She needed to get Chris alone.

"Would you like some coffee?" She offered, hoping that he had other things to do.

"No thank you." Billy rested his hands on his belt. "I have a ton of paperwork back at the office, and we need to plan another search between now and spring." He patted Chris's shoulder. "I'll be back." He turned and hobbled down the steps, making his way back to his cruiser. Gripping the door handle, he looked back up at Chris. The air felt electric, and Kelcy watched the men speak in silent code. She didn't have time to worry about what they were up to and headed for the kitchen table. Kelcy listened to the sound of Billy's cruiser pulling down the drive, and the clomp of Chris's steps, pausing just before the door. When he entered the kitchen and sat, the stress was evident on his face. His eyes looked heavy.

"What was that all about?" She pried, fiddling with the salt and pepper shakers, wondering if flying them around would pull her away from all of this.

"What was what?" He rested his elbows on the table.

"You and officer long-time-no-see out there." She cocked her head like a bird, her face twisting into exaggerated confusion. Chris leaned back and wiped his hands down the length of his face.

"He suspects foul play, Kelcy." He raised his eyebrows. A genuine look of shock straightened her face. "I told him that's all bullshit. She drowned, and he needed to leave that talk at the door. The only person with her was that little boy." He pointed toward the living room. "And there was no fucking way he did that." She put her head in her hands.

"I'm sorry," she said into the table. "I saw you two quietly talking, and I just assumed." Chris rolled his eyes and gave her a dismissive wave. "My dad is on his way here." Her voice echoed off the tabletop. Chris leaned in with a flat expression.

"What?" he clicked the last syllable between his tongue and teeth.

Kelcy looked up, fear turning her face pale. "I told him I found the cans, and he said he was on his way." Chris jumped from his seat and started pacing the kitchen. He shook his finger at her, his eyes wide in panic.

"I never mentioned you, Chris." She held her hand up. He nodded and continued to shake his finger. "I need you to calm down. He will be here in a few hours, and I need you focused and hidden." Chris stopped, giving her a puzzled look.

"I don't know what he is going to..." Her throat seized, cutting off her sentence. Chris pulled his chair next to her and sat down, placing his hand on her forearm. He stared at the table and then focused his eyes on her.

"I got you, okay." He squeezed her arm. She stood, pulling his arm with her. He hobbled up as she folded forward, wrapping her arms around his neck. Her warmth radiated into his chest, and he closed his eyes. Feeling their legs being squeezed, they both looked down. Seth had wrapped his arms around them, hugging their knees, his mop of brown hair nestled between their thighs. Chris rubbed the top of the boy's head. "Everything will be alright," Chris whispered.

Chapter 18: Confession

I don't know how babe. You called for me, and I am here.

Kelcy slowly extended her hand toward the void. Her arm trembling from her fingertips to her shoulder.

"I called you," she whispered.

Is he okay? Are you okay?

Kelcy stared into the blackness of her bedroom.

"We are not okay Bradley." The words snaked into the abyss, echoing off walls. There was a static hum in the silence that vibrated against her eardrums. There was a faint smell of rot. She could feel a presence circling her bed against the shadow's edge. She closed her eyes, picturing the Seattle apartment.

"You can't leave Kelcy." His voice slid between reality and the void.

The shadows folded in, wrapping around her, hugging her form. Kelcy wept as the familiar scent of his skin prickled her nostrils. *I am here.* He whispered, his voice caressing her cheek.

She closed her eyes and let the phantom engulf her.

"Why can't we leave?" she sobbed.

His breath hissed over her neck, climbing into her ear.

I have heard her, Kelcy. She is here with me. You don't need to run.

"Who is there?" She asked, squeezing her eyes tight as her heart thumped in unison with his breathing.

She is here, Kelcy, and she can bring us together. Listen to the lake.

"What?" Kelcy opened her eyes, panic rising in her throat.

His voice twisted, merging something deep and wet. *You need to go to her. Go to the shore.* He urged her.

"No!" She pushed the sheets from her body and crawled to the edge of the bed. The darkness hugged her, pulling her back to the center of the bed.

Don't you want to be together? He pleaded.

"It took Becky." She balled up her fists. "Why did it take her?"

Kelcy placed her foot on the cold floor and, with a hard tug, she broke from his embrace and rushed toward the door.

Babe, I came back for us. His voice became desperate. *Take our son to the lake before it's too late! Please!*

Kelcy slammed her back against the door and watched as the void faded, the shadows on her bed climbing toward the ceiling.

It always returns what it has been given, Kelcy. And soon, it will be too late. Bradley's voice slid away into the floorboards.

She pressed her back against the door; those words climbing from her memory accompanied by the smell of candy. Kelcy reached over and flicked the light switch. The room illuminated, pushing the darkness back to the corners and into the walls of the cabin. Her breath hitched when his presence dissolved, receding into a memory. "I'm sorry. I can't." She slumped to the floor with tears streaming down her face.

Chris lay motionless on the couch as Kelcy crept past him and entered the dark kitchen. She approached the door and looked out over the lake.

She is here with me. His voice slithered from the recesses of her mind.

Police tape fluttered from bent sticks in the sand, glowing against the deep blue of the moonlight. Kelcy didn't know who Bradley was referring to, and a coldness gripped her spine as her mind scrambled for the answer. When the information merged, the stupidity of not connecting the dots sooner made Kelcy's ears hot. The answer was in her great-granddad's letter. She had been on the ice that day. Taken the vacationers, leaving him to live with what had been done. What her family kept hidden. And now, she came here with her son and awakened her. Is that what Robert meant when he told her to listen?

Yes. His voice whispered behind her right ear. An intense feeling of sorrow fell over Kelcy as she watched the waves chop at the shore. It has been trying to tell her ever since she arrived. On the road that day, before Chris showed up. In the shadows of her room at night. The lake was trying to tell her about Sophia. But why did she take Becky? Kelcy felt something grip her stomach and twist.

She did not take your friend. Robert's voice crawled up her backside and rested on her shoulders. *It is your son. He has the sickness.*

Kelcy squeezed her eyes shut, fear gripping her chest. She pushed against Robert's voice.

"No." she shook her head, balling her fists. "He is just a little boy." The room spun in her peripheral as darkness pressed into the corners of her eyes.

Kelcy, you must listen to the lake. Robert begged. *This will not stop until you listen. Until you hear it. You have to sever the line.*

Kelcy pressed her fists against her temples and slammed her head into the door. The room spun as she collapsed to the floor. Robert faded into the hallway as a vignette of darkness engulfed her.

When Chris found her, he looked her over before picking her up and carrying her to the living room. He sat on the sofa chair, biting his thumbnail until the sun shot spears against the floor. He wanted to call an ambulance and decided against it, knowing full well they would take her away. They may even take Seth. If she seems unstable. That boy was her life, and he couldn't let that happen. She came to and sat up on the couch in a daze. She claimed she went to the kitchen to get a glass of water and became overtaken by a dizzy spell, blaming the incident on stress. Chris tried to show as little doubt as possible. He knew she was hiding information, but it wasn't the time to start an argument. He would start one later, when things calmed down. Seth waddled out and jumped on his mother's belly, yelling that he wanted toast. Kelcy hugged her son and ran her fingers through his hair. Everything seemed back to normal, but he warned her that if the dizziness returned, she needed to say something. She rolled her eyes and agreed to satisfy his false sense of authority. They spent the rest of the morning scanning the lake as the divers scoured the shoreline. The police would regroup on the beach, shake their heads, and then wave for the men to reenter the lake. By mid afternoon, they packed up for the day, leaving the bright yellow tape as a reminder that Becky was still missing. Kelcy spent time with Seth and Chris before dinner, sitting absent minded in front of the television. There was little, if no, conversation. When Kelcy put Seth to bed that evening, she brewed coffee and sat with Chris on the couch. They would need to make a plan before her father arrived. It was only a three-hour drive and she wasn't sure when he was arriving, but assumed he was well on his way by now. When Chris fell asleep, Kelcy figured it would be safer to have him here on the couch in case her father arrived in the middle of the night. She walked to the kitchen and stood at the front door, staring into the darkness of the lake. Kelcy pictured the little girl drifting in the tide. *You need to sever the line.* She looked back at the glow of the living room. Wicked imagery crawled its way forward, spiking her anxiety. What did Robert mean, sever the line? Was he asking her to kill her father?

Kelcy looked east to west, tracing the road, circling the lake. The shoreline looked serene. Its teeth, nipping at the edges and eating the sand.

"You ok?" Chris mumbled.

His voice cracked the silence, and Kelcy spun around, her heart fluttering in her chest. Chris stood under the living room archway, rubbing his forehead.

"Yeah, couldn't sleep." She put her hand on her stomach. "You scared the shit out of me."

"Sorry?" He walked to the table and slid into a seat. "What time is it?"

Kelcy looked at the stovetop clock.

"Two am." She looked back out toward the lake. Chris nodded and ran his hand through his hair and leaned his elbows on the table. Across the lake, two small orbs floated around the west side of the shoreline.

He's coming. The voice slithered from the base of her gut.

The small specks of light faded in and out as they hovered in the darkness.

"He's coming." She turned to Chris. He stood up and rubbed his eyes to wake himself up. "Okay, I need to get ready." Chris said as he crossed the kitchen and looked out toward the ebbing eyes.

"I'll hide in the bathroom." He turned.

She grabbed his forearm. "No." She said, "Go to the basement."

Chris huffed, put his hands on his waist, and looked around the room. He didn't think the basement was a suitable place to hide, but he needed to trust her.

"I'm going to stand ready behind that door." He pointed. Kelcy looked toward the basement and returned her gaze.

"Ok." She bit her bottom lip. Kelcy went to the cupboard and pulled two cups. "He will be here in about thirty minutes, give or take." Chris nodded and sat back down at the table, fidgeting with the salt and pepper shakers. Kelcy opened the bag of coffee grounds and ran the water in the kitchen sink. Chris put on a fake smile and pointed at the coffeemaker.

"Black please."

Chapter 19: Sins of the Father

Mathew Beckles was born into wealth. The kind of money that allowed him to pick his morality. When Grandpa Josephus died, his father sold the fishery. The cabin remained in their family, and he liquidated everything else, down to the little rowboat that Mathew questioned the ownership of. The ins and outs of the exchange, conducted on the phone over the course of a few days, guaranteed his family would never go without. His mother and father would drag him, kicking and screaming, to the cabin during the summer for visits. It was dull, the only refuge from complete boredom being the brief moments when he would sit on his grandad's lap and eat water toffee. The old man didn't talk a lot. But when he did, he would ramble on about the fishery and the Russians. Most of the time, he would stare out at the lake like he was waiting for something. His father would spend his time in the backyard reading, or on the phone in their bedroom. The time at the cabin was supposed to be for relaxing, not for business, and Mother would reiterate that whenever they were around each other. He would dismiss her, waving his hand, retreating into the bedroom or backyard. Mother would curse under her breath. Her lips twisted obscenities. He would have paid anything to hear her say them out loud. The shocked expression on his father's face as she told him what she thought of his bullshit. They hated each other. Only staying together on his behalf. When he was younger, he harbored a sense of guilt, but now, being married himself, he understood it. Marriage is hard. Maintaining a peaceful and conducive household takes a lot of energy, and children can exacerbate any present tensions. There were days when his boredom became unbearable. It lulled him into an oblivious black hole. When claustrophobia reared its ugly head, he would go for long walks around the lake. His father would stop whatever he was doing and remind him of the rules. His fascination with the lake was strange. Each season, during the drive, his father would repeat what he considered the most important thing for Mathew to remember. The rules. His mouth contorted in the rearview as he reinforced each one. Rule number one.

"Never wander into the woods. It's a dangerous place, Mathew." His father would tilt his head back, raising his voice to ensure he had his son's full attention. Rule number two.

"Under no circumstances are you to talk to the neighbor." His father would pause, staring out the corner of his eyes, while somehow keeping the car in their lane. Mathew would shake his head and look past his father at the oncoming traffic. He thought the old Native American man was harmless, and his dad was just being a racist. There would be a pause when he would mention the last and most important rule. His parents would hold each other's hands and his father would look back at him with a stoic expression. Rule number three. His voice would harden.

"You stay away from that lake, Mathew."

That's it. Stay away from the lake. It didn't matter if that rule made any sense. The rules, especially that one, were non-negotiable. Mathew thought it was stupid. The whole point of going to the cabin was that lake. A place to relax. Swim. Fish. When he was far enough away from his parents, he would stand at the shoreline and watch the tide snake up to his feet. There was something about the way it looked and not his dad's warning that kept him from stripping to his underwear and jumping in. He walked the shoreline, the edge of his sneakers grazing the wet sand, pulling his foot back just before the foam would bite.

The old man who lived next door sat in his rocking chair every day, at the end of his drive, eating hard candy. Mathew would tiptoe near the shore, pretending not to notice the old man as he passed the property. His old metal chair would squeak as he shifted his weight back and forth. Mathew wondered if all the old people around here owned an old worn out chair. Mathew would pass his drive and the sweet smell of hard candy made his mouth water, but he remembered rule number two. His father would kill him. He said the old man was a weirdo. The kind that likes kids a little too much. When the cabin became Mathew's, he brought his family, telling his daughter to stay away from the man as well. He always thought his father was a terrible man for treating the man with such disdain. His attitude changed when they arrived the first day and the old man was still alive, rocking in his chair. He waved at them as the faint creak cascaded across the lake. It creeped Mathew out, and he wondered if the geezer wasn't immortal. His skin looked like worn leather and his solid black eyes seemed to float in his sunken sockets. Lit with something magical. A power allowing him to steal your soul.

There was only one exchange between the man and his father. Mathew stopped in the road near the end of his property to tie his shoe. The old man watched him as he rocked back and forth. His father came out into the yard and descended the drive, stopping at the border of their property. With his toes teetering over the perfectly cut grass.

"Don't be talking to my boy, Robert. You understand me!" He yelled, pointing his finger.

The old man ignored him and turned his attention to the water. That night at the dinner table, when he asked his father why he yelled like that, his father slammed his hand down, rattling the silverware. Mathew's cup toppled over and juice poured over the edge of the table, making a patting sound against the hardwood floor. His mother went to the sink and grabbed a kitchen towel, shooting him a nasty look. His father ignored her, closing his eyes and taking a deep breath.

"There are some people that don't know how to mind their own business." He looked at his plate, a grimace spreading across his visage. "And that old codger is one of them."

The conversation ended with his mother saying, "Think we can have one dinner without an outburst?" She finished wiping up the juice, sitting back in her seat, and smiling at her son. His father nodded, wiping his hands on his napkin before standing up, shaking his head, and walking off into the living room. The television crackled to life and a news reporter rambled on about politics while they finished their meal in silence.

Years later, he understood what his father meant about the old man. Robert was there in the shadows, watching. Hidden by the enormous tree looming over his property. The day he lost his temper. The day he killed that boy. He was there when Mathew put the boy in the lake, repeating what his grandfather had done years before. What his father concealed in a red coffee can. Would his father be proud of him? Keeping the trophies of their curse. What he now must preserve. Would Kelcy understand what lived in the lake? The curse their family endured. The reason he kept the old man Robert at arm's length. She only spoke to him once, and like his father before him, he hovered at the end of their property and pointed, reminding the man to keep to his own. Kelcy pretended to stay away. Her father stood vigil the first few times she passed Robert's home. The old man rocked in his chair, ignoring his daughter as he was told to. Mathew thought Robert would be there, rocking in that chair, eating candy, long after their bloodline was dead and gone. He fantasized about killing the old coot, but there was a fear that swelled in his crotch. Something told him never to dare it. When his father showed him the can. What his grandfather Josephus collected. Mathew asked his father if he had ever killed anyone? His father smiled and patted his head, saying, for whatever reason, the curse skipped him.

"We have a curse?" Mathew asked.

His father squeezed his shoulder, hardening his expression.

"We will talk another time, Mathew. When you're ready."

He lay in bed that night, the shadows dancing on the ceiling, as he imagined what it meant to have a curse. How special it was. Would it skip him, too? He listened to the grunts of his parents. The cries of pain from his mother. He wondered if his dad lied about being skipped. He would listen to her plead and beg. The slaps and thuds, followed by muffled moans, through their old wooden floorboards. Mathew's crotch would swell, and he squeezed it until pain radiated up into his throat. They all bear some type of curse, whether or not they accept it.

Robert understood it. Mathew witnessed it reflected in his black orbs. The curves of his mouth. His frown, blaming and calling them out. His father never allowed him near that lake, and that rule remained. Until Kelcy arrived. As Mathew grew older, the stories of a family curse became nothing more than folklore nonsense. He never once felt the urge to kill. Until that day. Lakes are not evil. People are. He remembered his father saying that old man Robert liked children a little too much. He always wondered about the validity of the statement, but he kept his daughter at arm's length, just in case. Then he had dumped the boy into its mouth. Fear overrode his common sense. His attention to detail. He disappointed his father. Allowing Robert to witness their family's secret. Now the threat seemed more visceral. His curse had finally manifested. The sickness of his bloodline passed down? The shadows of his abyss were deeper and darker now. There was a smell under the foam that washed the shore. Even the ice looked vicious in its serenity. The old man Robert didn't inform the authorities, once again, allowing us to feed the host of the land. He was a sentinel, wasn't he? A gatekeeper. Mathew understood full well what the old man Robert was here to do. A witness to the curse passed down from father to son. Was Robert waiting for something? Some type of incantation? Something to summon the lake to swallow them whole? Was there a pact between him and the abyss? This was the reason they needed to stay away from the water. The reason he needed to keep his child away from Robert and that Godforsaken lake.

He never wanted a child, but his wife insisted. His mother showed no signs of the curse, so when his wife gave birth to a girl, Mathew thought it would skip a generation. If his daughter chose to have a family, he prayed her children were girls. Sparing his daughter and grandchild. Did it skip the females, or did his mother and daughter show it differently, like his father? The self-destructive nature of their choices. When Kelcy married a drug addict, bringing a child into this world as a bastard, Mathew considered the child's fate. Birthing a boy brought the possibility of their curse. He would need to teach the boy. Show him the gifts. What if his daughter refused? He would need to ensure her cooperation. Or end this all himself. Not at the lake. He couldn't put his child and grandson there.

Mathew turned the west corner of the lake and headed down the narrow dirt road towards the cabin. There was a lot to discuss. A lot to explain. Decisions to make. Many things for Kelcy to understand. The woods to his right twisted in his peripheral, washing into the darkness of his rearview. The lake glimmered against the moon as he sped along the lakeside. Mathew rubbed his eyes, awakening his senses. He would need to prepare himself for the actions he might be forced to take. What his bloodline expected. He had to be strong and focused. The lights of the cabin came into view as two specks on the horizon, disappearing in and out of the trees as he rounded the west bend of the lake.

Chapter 20: Old Friends

They sat at the table in complete silence, waiting to hear the familiar crunch of tires come up the drive. Her anxiety wrapped itself around her throat and yanked.

Babe, you need to calm down. Bradley's voice crept up her spine.

Kelcy held her breath as she pushed his voice to the back of her head. Chris sipped his coffee and thumbed the rim as he opened and closed his mouth a few times. Like he wanted to say something.

You need to bring him to the water, Kelcy. Before your father gets here.

Kelcy closed her eyes, rolling them into the back of her head in pain. His voice was digging, tearing at the fabric of her sanity. She couldn't do this right now. Her father was arriving at any moment. She wasn't bringing her son anywhere near that lake.

I can protect him, Kelcy. She is here, and Becky is too. His voice pleaded.

Becky's name made Kelcy's stomach twist. Bile churned its way up her throat and she clenched her jaw, swallowing, pushing it back down. The taste burned. Kelcy stood up and excused herself to check on Seth. Chris nodded and sipped his coffee, looking out toward the porch. He wasn't sure what was going to happen when he saw him again. Chris only knew it was going to be hard not to beat the man to a pulp. Memories of his brother flooded forward. Mark would smack him in the head when he messed up a client's yard. Ignoring him when he tried to follow Mark and his girlfriend of the week to the mall. The time his big stupid brother had saved him from that oversized inbred bully, Kelly Jacobs. Chris smiled as he wiped his eyes and nursed his cup.

Kelcy watched Seth's chest rise and fall. There was an intense fear of her father growing in the pit of her stomach. Knowing that man did that to Mark. Her great-grandfather murdered that little girl. Were they in danger now that she knew? Fear pulsed through her entire body, and it screamed for her to run.

"What are you going to do with our son?" she asked the voice. Her words echoed in the hallway and she held her breath, waiting for him to answer. There was a calmness in his voice she hadn't expected. A tone that had once been desperate now sounded serene.

I will make sure he is safe, Kelcy. We will keep him safe. Away from your father. The voice slithered forward.

Kelcy clenched her fists as she exhaled. The air in her lungs ran out, and she gasped, opening and closing her fists. Taking deep breaths to calm herself. What was she going to do? If her father had made plans to hurt them, she would need to rely on Chris to protect them. Would he be able to? Would he kill for them? As much as she trusted him, she wasn't sure he could follow through with that. The idea of her father's rage manifesting in front of her son made her sick. Would he kill her first and make him watch?

"Okay," she whispered. "Let me get Chris into the basement." She looked at her hands and squeezed them together, trying to stop them from shaking.

Hurry, the voice hissed as it huddled at the base of her neck. *He is almost here.*

Kelcy looked down at Seth and covered her mouth as tears welled, blurring her vision. She straightened her posture and with a deep inhale;

coughed into the crook of her arm, wiped her eyes, and headed out to the kitchen. Chris was nursing his cup, his eyes swollen with a hard sadness. *What if he can't?* She thought again. He looked up at Kelcy and grinned. She would need to trust Bradley now.

"You okay?" he asked, noticing her hands. Kelcy rubbed them together and shook her head, looking out toward the porch.

"You need to get to the basement now." She took his cup and placed it in the sink. Chris gave her a stern look and leaned in, placing his hands on the table.

"I wasn't finished with that," he tried to joke.

Kelcy turned and gave him a gesture to get up.

"Did you see his car out the window or something?" He approached the little window in the front door and peered out into the darkness of the yard.

"I want to be ready, Chris. Please." She asked. The last word had a commanding tone to it, and Kelcy closed her eyes in regret, hoping she didn't just ruin his cooperation. He nodded and put his hands up, walking toward the basement door. Kelcy exhaled and opened it in relief as she backed away.

"I'll call you when he arrives, okay?" She put on a fake smile and averted her eyes to the floor. Chris nodded and entered the stairwell. Cold air mixed with the faint smell of mold flushed up from the depths. He hobbled down a few steps before looking back up. Kelcy closed the door, and he listened to her footsteps retreating to the back room again.

She wrapped Seth in a blanket and shushed him when he moaned, tucking him to her chest. She passed the living room, pausing in the kitchen to stare at the basement door. Her face felt hot. After everything he had done for her, she left him to uncertainty in a basement.

Hurry, Bradley's voice stabbed. *He is almost here!*

Kelcy laid Seth on the table and walked to the front door. Peering out, she let her eyes adjust to the darkness. To her left, small amber lights bounced in the distance. Bradley was right. Kelcy gripped the door and turned the handle, freezing when it made a loud click. She looked back at the basement door, waiting for Chris to call out. When he didn't, she swung the door open, scooped up her son, and stepped out into the cold. The air bit her face as she shut the door behind her. Tiny silver orbs danced in the air, falling into the thin curtain of snow in the yard.

"Kelcy?" Chris called from the depths of the house. She squeezed her son to her chest and looked over the porch railing. She needed to hurry. Kelcy ascended the steps, grabbing the railing with one hand to steady herself as Seth moaned against her. She kissed the top of his head and made her way into the yard.

"We are going to see Daddy, Peapod." She cooed, heading down the drive toward the beach.

The darkness of the void confused her senses, pulling her back and forth within the small gusts of snow. Waves in the distance hissing her forward. The glow of teeth eating the sand gave her direction, and she approached the water's edge, staring into the mouth of the lake.

"Bradley?" she whispered.

The water held a black gaze. The tide beckoned her closer, whispering her name.

Kelcy, I'm here, baby. Come closer. His voice cooed.

Her heart felt heavy as she stepped into the water. Wading out, the freezing essence of its soul climbed her legs, gripping her, not allowing her to move. She panicked, her pulse racing, pounding in the corners of her vision. The void of the water swallowed the falling white orbs, cracking the sheets of ice that scaled its shore behind her.

We are here, Kelcy, hold him out to us.

She hugged Seth tighter, fear swallowing her whole. Her grip constricted as she clenched her eyes shut.

Kelcy! Robert's voice swirled in the wind.

Kelcy squeezed harder. A soft moan creaked from her chest as she trembled.

Kelcy, we are here. Let us save the boy. Bradley begged. A faint female voice swirled, echoing behind him. Another ebbed forward from the depths of the lake. A frail child mimicking the others.

"Becky?" Kelcy called out, gripping Seth tighter. The voices penetrated her mind, pulling at her sanity.

"Stop it!" Kelcy screamed. She gripped her triceps and squeezed, her nails digging into the fabric of her shirt.

Kelcy! Robert called from behind her. *STOP!*

A loud popping sound split the air, and she froze, opening her eyes to the chopping current. The waves rocked back and forth, making her wobble.

Robert stood on the small cresting shore, his black orbs filled with immense sadness. Kelcy loosened her arms and looked down at her son's sagging body. An inhuman scream bellowed from her throat as she collapsed in the shallow. Laughs trickled across the top of the water and Kelcy shook her head back and forth.

"NO, NO, NO!" His head rolled to the side as she hugged him.

Robert watched as she rocked her child, the waves crashing over them, white froth hugging their dark forms.

Kelcy, Robert looked out over the lake. *The dead play tricks, child. This is your family's curse. You need to end it. It needs to end with your father. You need to set them free.* He pointed his blackened finger to the depths. He lifted his hand toward the sky. His aura vibrated.

Within the trees. Within the land. It tried to whisper your family's secrets. It tried to warn you.

Kelcy screamed as she hugged her son's limp body. Robert turned and walked into the darkness. Into the depths of the void. Disappearing under the waves. Kelcy screamed to him, reaching her arm out, and grabbing into the falling white orbs.

It ends with your father. His voice faded into the ether.

Give her to me now. The voices contorted back and forth from Bradley's to Becky, and then the child. A gurgle that ebbed in the foam, wet and dead, climbed and pulled at them. Kelcy shook her head.

What will you do with him now, Kelcy? Put him in a can? That's no place for a little boy. They laughed.

Kelcy shuffled to her feet. Opening her mouth wide, a guttural cry emanated from her dry throat, cascading across the surface of the lake. Her son's lifeless head bobbed back and forth as the foaming teeth gnawed at her shins. A darkness swirled from beneath the waves a few feet from where she stood. Veins appeared within their crests, and Kelcy tried to step back, panic rising, locking her knees. They snaked through the water, wrapping themselves around her ankles. Kelcy tried to kick her legs out and lost her balance, toppling over into the shallow water. She felt the tendrils tighten around her ankles and pull her deeper into the lake. She spread her arms out and dug her fingers into the clay of the lake bed. The tendrils let her go and she jerked up from under the water, sputtering and coughing. Kelcy rose to her feet and wobbled in the knee high water. She waded back to the shore as vomit raced up her throat and mixed with the foam that circled her feet. Horror twisted her face as she looked at her empty hands. A horrific scream cut the hissing of the shoreline as she collapsed onto the beach.

Chapter 21: What happened to Mark?

His backside hurt from sitting on the narrow wooden steps leading to the basement. He shifted his weight, trying to find comfort in such a cramped space. Chris perked his ears and listened for Kelcy to give him the go ahead, ready to spring into action. He had a plan worked out, and whether or not Kelcy would agree with it was of no concern now. *It's a little late for that conversation.* Once he was in front of the man, he would punch him square in the face. Put him down. Kelcy would hate him for a very long time, if not indefinitely, and he would relent once her father confessed. Chris wanted an explanation. Why he had killed his brother? The sound of gravel crunching made him lift his weight off the step and climb closer to the door. His legs were throbbing, and he rubbed his palms against his thighs to wake them up. Chris leaned his ear against the door and slowed his breathing. There was the sound of a slamming door followed by footsteps on the porch stairs. His heart started racing. He positioned himself, ready to burst through the basement door. This was it. His hands were shaking, and he felt the sudden urge to throw up. The front door opened, and the footsteps stopped inside the doorway. The wind blew across the hardwood floor, seeping under the basement door, cooling the sweat that now dripped like a faucet down the sides of his face.

"Kelcy?" a man's voice called, taking a few steps into the cabin. The front door closed with a loud slam as the footsteps moved past the kitchen and into the living room. Chris placed his hands on the walls of the staircase and adjusted his position. He waited for the steps to disappear into the back of the house before he opened the door and peeked out. Chris listened to her father shuffle around in the back of the house and made his way to the kitchen table. He lifted a chair, putting it down as slowly as possible. He sat down and positioned himself as if he were lounging. When Mathew stepped into the kitchen, he froze, staring in bewilderment. Chris smiled and folded his arms across his chest to conceal his shaking hands as her father tilted his head. His realization of the stranger's identity spread across his face and he turned the corners of his mouth up. His eyes looked as if they were vibrating in the soft glow of the room.

"Christopher!" he placed his hands into his front pockets and leaned his weight to one leg. "My, it has been a long time," he looked up to the ceiling and then turned his eyes down, squinting. "Since the disappearance of your brother, right?" A wicked smile spread across his face, showing only his top teeth. Chris felt his heart pounding in his chest. Rage blinded him as he burst from his position, almost knocking the table over. Mathew pulled his hand from his pockets and held them up, chest level, in surrender. "Easy son," he took a step back. "There is no need for violence." Chris took a step forward, his fists balled at his sides.

"I am not your fucking son," Chris spat, opening and closing his hands. Mathew bowed his head and patted the air. "Understood," he said in a calming tone. "I am looking for my daughter. You seen her?" He widened his smile.

Chris loosened his fists. "She's not in the cabin?" He cocked his head in confusion, fear prickling his spine. In all the excitement and anger, Chris realized her father was standing in the kitchen and Kelcy was nowhere to be found. He would have dragged her out of hiding. Where was Seth? Mathew shook his head and Chris turned, looked out the little window into the darkness, and stared back at Mathew. Panic overrode his anger as his mind raced.

"What did you do, Christopher?" Mathew asked, tilting his head. Chris turned and opened the door, stepping out onto the porch. He cupped his hands and called her name, the wind swallowing his voice into the void. The snow fell like a curtain, obscuring the beach.

"Maybe we should call the police?" Mathew asked with a mock concern in his voice, laughing as Chris scanned the yard. His rage returned, swelling behind his eyes, and Chris turned and pointed at Mathew.

"If anything has happened to them, I am going to kill you." He raised his voice.

Mathew placed his hand on his chest and made a surprised face, hyper-extending his jaw open.

Foam formed at the corner of Chris's mouth. "You killed my brother, you piece of shit." He stepped back.

Mathew dropped his hand and shook his head. "Small town Saturday night, son," he frowned. "Lots of stories over the years. You sure I killed him and not some angry dad?"

Chris bolted across the room and kicked the closest kitchen chair. It hit the stove; the legs snapping off and skirting across the hardwood floor. "

I saw the can you sick fuck!" he yelled.

Mathew's smile faded, and he lowered his hands. Chris stepped toward him, and Mathew went to the counter and pulled a knife from the butcher block. Chris backed up and felt his heart drop. They hadn't discussed the fact that her father knew where everything was in this cabin, and now that he looked around the room, there were plenty of things he could use to his advantage. Mathew smiled and held the blade out.

"That story will never be told." He squeezed the handle.

"Do you know why I killed him, Chris, hmm?" Mathew stepped to the kitchen table. "I caught him." Chris balled his fists and walked to the opposite side, keeping his distance. "He assumed we were gone that day," Mathew smiled and continued. "But I had returned for my wife's sunglasses." He tapped the tip of the knife off the tabletop. Anxiety gripped Chris by his throat as he watched him play with the blade. "When I walked into our bedroom and saw your brother standing by the dresser, I figured I could understand some of what he was thinking. After all, I used to listen to my parents fuck, and sometimes, it was exhilarating." His head swam as he listened to Kelcy's father. His thoughts raced, trying to figure out his next move as Mathew continued the story. "But panties weren't all he found, was it?" Mathew gripped the handle of the knife and raised it to eye level. "He found my family secret." He made a ticking sound with his tongue and sucked air through his pursed lips. "So, I did what needed to be done, Christopher." Chris wiped the tears forming in his eyes. Snot had dripped down his upper lip, and Mathew gave him a pitiful look. "Don't be angry, Chris. I did you a favor. Imagine if this were to have gotten out!" He waved the blade through the air. "Mark, the pervert of Cossayuna!" He raised his voice, yelling the title like a Shakespearean actor. "I did you a favor," he repeated, lowering his voice, his eyes piercing. "Your family would have suffered more than mine. After all, who is going to believe some punk ass kid that mows lawns and gawks at underage girls?"

Chris grabbed the edge of the table and flipped it over, knocking Mathew backward. He rushed forward, grabbing Mathew's hand and seizing the knife above his head. He punched her father in the stomach and Mathew heaved in a wide-eyed stare. Chris struck him again on the side of the head and Mathew doubled over, hitting the floor with a thud. As Chris grabbed the back of his shirt, Mathew swung his arm around and sliced Chris across the ribcage. He howled and backed away, blood speckling the hardwood. Mathew held his stomach and let out a horrendous laugh. Chris looked toward the porch and gave the middle finger before flinging the door open and plunging out, disappearing into the void. The white sheet of snow falling beyond the porch blinded Mathew as he stood in the ruins of the kitchen. He stretched his back, moaning to the ceiling.

"I always hated that fucking kid," he scowled and walked out onto the porch, frowning as he watched Chris's silhouette head down the drive.

Chris swung his arms out, trying to keep his balance as he rushed away from the cabin. He navigated the drive, now covered in a thin sheet of ice. His ribcage burned and the cold air licked his wound, sending spires of pain up his side. He needed to find Kelcy. Up ahead, the beach faded into view and Chris paused, sliding a few feet before coming to a complete stop. He wasn't sure if his eyes were playing tricks. There was something on the beach near the water. It looked like a body. He leaned forward, shadowing his eyes with his hand.

"Kelcy?" he called out, his voice cracking against the blowing swirls of snow.

He stared at the black form, watching for movement, and inched a few steps closer. He looked back at the cabin. The silhouette of her father cut the light from the open porch door, its rays searing the void like a beacon. Chris rushed forward. As he approached the shoreline, he found Kelcy lying face down in the sand. Her clothes were soaked and there was no sign of Seth. Chris rolled her over and put his head to her chest. Her faint heartbeat thumped against his ear.

"Kelcy?" He held her face in his hands and turned her head back and forth, trying to elicit a response.

The panic in his voice elevated when he looked back and didn't see her father on the porch. "Kelcy, where is Seth?" He held her head in one hand and tried to pry one of her eyelids open. "Kelcy!" he shook her. Chris lay her head down and stood up, scanning the shoreline.

"Seth!" He yelled, cupping his hands around his mouth. A searing pain brought him to his knees as Mathew pushed the knife into his lower back. Chris toppled forward into the shallow mouth of the lake. The icy water gripped his chest like a vise, stealing his breath. Mathew raised the blade above his head and clenched his teeth. A form appeared from the flurry a few yards out in the lake and Mathew paused, staring wide-eyed as the shape of a man faded into view. He seemed to hover above the water like an apparition. Mathew blinked a few times and stumbled back away from Chris. A limb extended from the form, its dark appendages curling into a fist and then extending one finger. The face of the shadow cut through the blinding snow and Mathew gasped as the visage of the old man appeared before him.

What you give the lake, it returns, Mathew. His voice was wet, each syllable crackling like an old radio. *Your family has brought evil to this lake, and it has cursed you in return.*

Mathew clenched the knife in his fist and looked back at Kelcy's lifeless form.

You gave it death. The old man floated closer. *And now, it shall return death to you.*

Mathew scoffed and raised the knife above his head and advanced toward Chris.

"Well," he screamed, his eyes bulging with rage. "Let me give it another."

Chris turned over and raised his hand in defense, the water splashing over his face. He could feel something slide past him, and he screamed under the water as the fractured reflection of her father ebbed above him.

Mathew swung the blade down and, in an instant, he was swept off his feet. He lost his grip on the knife and it swirled away as he slammed on his side in the shallow water. The frozen sheet cut into his arm and he could smell his blood as it painted the white frost crimson. He sat up and looked out toward the old man. He pointed his finger and opened his mouth wide. His eyes locked onto the approaching wave as the horror of the lake strangled his scream. Black tendrils swirled in and out of the crest, riding the foam. A faint whisper emanated from the wind.

Leave his brother alone.

He covered his face as the spirit swirled from the wave, crashing into him and dragging him out into the lake.

The lake calmed. Snow drifted onto its surface, mixing with its body. Chris crawled up the beach and collapsed next to Kelcy. He placed his hand on her chest and held his breath. Her heart beat against his palm, and he exhaled with a sigh of relief. He needed to find Seth.

He looked back over the lake. The glass surface reflected the falling snow and Chris saw a figure floating out in the shadows of the void. A little boy. His heart sank as the apparition waved and then faded into the flurry. The wind carried a familiar giggle. He closed his eyes as his emotions came forth like a flood. He huddled next to Kelcy, and he wept.

Chapter 22: Aftermath

When Bill pulled around the west end of the lake, he saw the flames above the treetops. There was no sense in turning on the sirens because there wasn't a soul that was out on these roads in this condition. Plus, there was no way anyone could save that cabin. Chris was sitting in his truck at the base of the driveway as the flames licked the trees at the edge of the yard. Kelcy lay unresponsive in the passenger seat, wrapped in a blanket. Billy called first responders from the next county over, as well as the fire department. Extra police came out from Greenwich to help with the blaze, securing the road on either side of the lake. He tried to pull Chris aside to ask him what happened, but his responses were incoherent. He rambled on about a girl in the lake.

In the official statement, taken two days later, Chris told Bill about the cans they found. Her father's involvement in the murder of his brother, and the attempt on his life at the lake. Her father was nowhere to be found. His car, damaged during the fire, left Billy with little to go on. Kelcy's son was missing, and when asked about the boy, Chris just shook his head. Billy questioned him again back at the precinct, getting very little information. He would give it some time. Billy assumed he was dead and hoped Chris would remember any information that might lead to the boy's body. Give his mother a chance to have some kind of closure. The state investigators seized the cans and towed away her father's car, leaving the rest of the carnage for Billy's department to clean up. Chris admitted to setting the fire to the cabin from the basement. He said it was a haunted place that needed to be destroyed. From the contents of the can, Billy couldn't say he would disagree.

Kelcy remained in the hospital for several weeks. She lost her right foot to frostbite and extreme hypothermia almost took her life. Her injuries would leave a physical reminder of that place. Billy took to visiting her every other day to check on her progress. He struggled, wondering if her survival was more a curse than a miracle. There was shame in that thought and he kept it to himself, but if he were in her shoes, he wouldn't want to survive his child. Haunted by the memories of what was. When he knocked on her door that morning, she sat up with a look on her face that told him she was ready to talk.

Billy took notes as she told him about her escape. How her father attacked Chris and her son. She didn't know where else to go, so she headed toward the lake. When her father stabbed Chris on the beach, she waded into the water out of fear. She lost her balance. Tears streamed down her face as she recalled losing her son to the lake. Billy noted the contradictions between hers and Chris's account, nodding as she recalled the details. Chris stated that when he fled from the cabin, he came upon her, lying on the beach. The boy was already missing. Billy had the burden of proof to deal with, and that was something he lacked. Either way, the story was tragic, and Billy couldn't assume foul play. She had paid enough.

The lake also claimed Kelcy's father. Chris said the water was rough, and that her father slipped on the ice. When he emerged from the lake, her father was gone.

"Slipped on ice?" Billy questioned.

Chris nodded. It was too early in the season for the lake to freeze over. Outside of the expected thin layer of primary ice, there was nothing to slip on. Billy took the notes and shook Chris's hand.

The local news covered the arson and her father's involvement in the murder of Mark Hume. Kelcy watched, anxiety squeezing her spine, paralyzing her senses. The hospital released her a few weeks later, and Billy asked her to stay in town in case there were any more questions. He put her up in a motel just outside of town, on his dime. She skipped out three days later, and he didn't bother pursuing her.

Chris healed from his injuries and received a five-year sentence for the arson. He admitted to setting the cabin on fire with fuel from the basement he found while inspecting the furnace and wood stove for Kelcy. During the sentencing, he said he would have done it sooner if he knew about what her father had done to Mark. He only wished the bastard was in there when he struck the match. Billy shook his head and let the kid pick his fate. Chris always did, even when they were kids.

During that summer, Billy brought the case to a close, and the county arranged for a demolition crew to clean up the site. Billy heard that Kelcy's mother committed suicide a few days after the news broke about her father. They tried to reach out to her, getting no response. Now he knew why. The whole thing was a mess. Old rumors about her great-grandad Josephus resurfaced as popular gossip. He did his best to shut it down when people brought it up around him, but folks were allowed to talk, even if it was distasteful. They did it back then, and they will do it now. The summer turned into fall and then crept into winter. The lake returned to its normal boring self, and Billy tried to stay away from that side of the lake as much as possible. If he drove by the vacant lot, he would look out over the lake until he passed. Billy made it a point to visit Chris once a month, but by late July, Chris denied visitation, and Billy, although hurt by his rejection, took it with a grain of salt. His old friend needed time to heal. Maybe, when he was released, they could meet up and have a beer far away from this place. The last time Billy looked at the files, he had laid them out across his desk and scanned over the documents and pictures. He thumbed through the images of the charred cabin and the worn expression on his friend's face in the court photos. The sadness in Kelcy's eyes in her hospital bed. There was a picture of her son taken at some point many years ago that Billy pulled from an online source. He might have been a year old in the photo. The young man holding him, Billy later learned, was Kelcy's husband Bradley. He passed away from addiction some years ago. No wonder her eyes carried such grief. It was too much pain for any one soul to harbor. He wondered where she was now. If she was alive, how the hell did she go on with it? Billy piled all documents in the box and closed the lid, carrying it over to his office closet and sliding the box onto the closed pile. He tapped the top of the box with his open palm. Closing the door, Billy gave himself a moment of silence. He shut off the light and closed the door to his office and to this chapter of the lake's dark history.

Chapter 23: What Lies Beneath

The cab pulled up next to the beach, and the driver looked in his rearview, giving the woman an odd look.

"You just want me to drop you here?" he smiled.

She grinned and handed a wad of cash over the back of the seat. He shrugged his shoulders and nodded as the woman balanced her crutches before climbing out. He waited for her to change her mind, and when Kelcy nodded and waved, he drove off. She waited for him to turn the bend before she faced the empty lot. She looked over at Robert's drive. The big sentinel swayed above his home, sending a creak across the lake, announcing her arrival. She walked down to the beach and stared at the glass surface of the water. Closing her eyes, she took in the lake's breath. The smell of sugar drifted over her shoulder and she bit into her tongue, waiting to hear his voice.

Why have you returned? Robert's voice swirled around her head.

Kelcy could feel him everywhere as fear gripped her, tightening around her body.

"I need him back, Robert." A sudden weight of sadness pressed against her chest as the voice drew closer.

Let him go, Kelcy. He is with us now. He whispered.

She pressed her teeth into the meat of her tongue, tasting her metallic ichor.

"What you give, it will return. Isn't that what you said?"

The form pulled away, and Kelcy spun around. Robert's face ebbed between her world and theirs, his visage appearing within gusts of wind. His black orbs wept for her.

It cannot return what you have lost. He extended his phantom arms and embraced her. She melted into the apparition, the sweet taste of sugar mixing with her tears as she wept with her friend.

He is with us now. Guarded and safe. The old man looked toward his sentinel, and Kelcy watched as the tree bent toward them, its limbs creaking in protest.

"Can I be with you too?" She asked.

Robert looked down at her and shook his head. *Not here, not now. But when it is your time, he will be here, waiting.*

He smiled and caressed her face with his eyes. Kelcy bowed her head and pulled away. Robert watched as she waded out into the lake, his smile fading as she drew the small knife from her pocket. She flipped its shiny tooth open and looked out over the void.

"I love you, Peapod." she whispered as the light danced against the steel.

Robert stretched out his arm, floating toward her with his mouth gaping in a scream. The sweet smell of sugar engulfed her senses as she swiped the blade across her wrist. Her crimson essence poured into the mouth of the lake as Robert burst into a million butterflies, their bright yellow wings ascending above her head like a cloud of magic. With shaky hands, Kelcy ran the blade over the other wrist and let out a moan.

What have you done? His voice faded into the void of the lake.

Black tendrils slithered across the surface of the water, and Kelcy smiled as they swirled around her waist. They climbed up her body as she turned her head up, closing her eyes to the sun. The black veins snaked into her mouth and she gagged as they slithered down her throat, filling her. Kelcy's organs hugged the tendrils, her blood mixing with the spirits of the lake. The limbs of the sentinel screamed as the wind rose. A rumble came from the void, dragging Kelcy under as she clawed at the crest of the wave. Robert stood at the edge of his dirt drive, holding Seth's hand.

Come, child, he whispered. Seth looked out over the lake, letting go of Robert's hand.

When will Mommy come back? He asked.

Robert stared at the calming water and looked down at the boy in silence. Seth twisted his upper lip and huffed, turning and heading up toward the old cabin. Becky stood in the rotting doorway and Seth picked up speed, running to her. She scooped him up, hugging him tight and kissing his cheek.

Mommy will be home soon kiddo. She smiled.

Mark stood under the sentinel and closed his eyes, listening to the lake whisper its secrets. Robert studied the shoreline. A little girl stood ankle-deep in the water, staring up at him, a wicked smile splitting her face. He could feel the pull of her wake, and he nodded at her. She turned and headed back into the deep, disappearing under a rippling tide. Robert looked back toward the cabin. Hopefully, Never, he wanted to tell the boy. But the lake always returns what's given.

About the Author

Andrien Beck lives with his wife and children in Diamond Point, New York.

Find him on Twitter/Instagram/Facebook

@AndrienBeck

www.ingramcontent.com/pod-product-compliance
Lightning Source LLC
LaVergne TN
LVHW012251070526
838201LV00108B/318/J

www.ingramcontent.com/pod-product-compliance
Lightning Source LLC
LaVergne TN
LVHW012251070526
838201LV00108B/318/J